THIS RAW, RED LAND

THIS RAW, RED LAND

Voncille Shipley

iUniverse, Inc.
New York Lincoln Shanghai

This Raw, Red Land

All Rights Reserved © 2003 by Voncille Shipley

No part of this book may be reproduced or transmitted in any form or by any means, graphic, electronic, or mechanical, including photocopying, recording, taping, or by any information storage retrieval system, without the written permission of the publisher.

iUniverse, Inc.

For information address:
iUniverse, Inc.
2021 Pine Lake Road, Suite 100
Lincoln, NE 68512
www.iuniverse.com

This book is a work of fiction. All names, characters, and incidents are either the product of the author's imagination or are used fictitiously except the name of the last Territorial Sheriff of Pickens County, Chickasaw Nation, Indian Territory—Thompson Pickens. All town names used are of actual places but are used fictitiously. Chagris had a post office from 1896 to 1909 but any other depiction of this town is fictitious.

ISBN: 0-595-27136-7

Printed in the United States of America

For my husband, John Shipley, who encouraged me to write it, and in memory of my parents, Jim and Emerine Emberling

1907

CHAPTER 1

Ben

Ben Conover had a hard time urging the horses up the incline. He didn't want to go in the first place and, too, sprouts had grown up in the trail he had hacked out just before he went back to Texas in January. He and Paul had slaved over the task and he failed to see why the family hadn't kept the lane clear. I don't think they're using it, he thought. I wonder why. Now on an airless midafternoon in late September in the year of our Lord nineteen-aught-seven, he and the horses, thirsty and tired, lagged the last few yards of their journey.

Feeling sweat trickling down his face, he took off his hat and wiped his brow on the rough homespun of his long shirtsleeve. A lock of mousy hair fell over his forehead. He brushed it back with a practiced forearm and replaced the sweat-stained felt hat. Best get out of the wagon so he could see the big rocks to throw them out of the lane rather than run over them. He jumped from the bed wincing from sore, stiff joints after the long journey and vowing to install a spring seat before traveling again.

Ben thought with dread of the coming involvement in his big, noisy family as he ambled back down the trail to the bend and looked back along the road. Broad of shoulder and lean of torso, he walked with a gait formed by long hours astride a mount and years of wearing cowboy boots. He took his hat off again and shaded his deep-set gray eyes with a work-roughened hand. Red dust raised by the passage of his wagon and team had resettled onto the surface; he had a clear view for at least a half-mile. Nothing moved in the humid air, not even a leaf of the dusty elms that formed a canopy over the road. Sun rays glinted red as they touched the dancing motes of dust.

Old Bob was nowhere in sight. Heaviness settled in his midsection at the realization he had lost Uncle Prent's best squirrel dog. When Old Bob had followed him, it had seemed the answer to his dilemma. He felt obliged to help his family get settled in Indian Territory but they expected him to stay permanently. His heart lay in his home state; he was a Texan born and bred. If Uncle Prent's dog followed him, a righteous man would return him, wouldn't he? Did it matter how long it took? So instead of running Bob off, he had whistled to him and patted the wagon-bed by his side.

The dog had stayed with him all the way from Texas until an hour or so after noon today. He had wandered off into the woods and did not return despite repeated calls and whistles. Ben had vacillated between taking his saddle horse to hunt the dog, leaving the team and wagon, or continuing on his journey hoping to find him later. Finally he had decided to leave Old Bob and proceed on his way.

Returning to his rig, Ben walked ahead of the team heaving rocks out of the way of the wheels, leading the horses. At the crest of the rise in a stand of blackjack trees, he paused and the team stood still behind him.

Directly in front of him a clearing sloped downward toward a creek. In its center stood a sixteen by twenty-foot log house shaded by several large pecan trees. Behind the house, log sheds, a brush arbor, and a half-dugout formed the essentials of a beginning farmstead. Fields of cotton flanked the house on either side stretching in quarter-mile long rows parallel to the creek. Last year when they moved to the Chickasaw Nation, he had helped with clearing land and erecting the buildings, but the family finished the house after he went back to Texas to work for Uncle Prent to finish paying for his wagon and team. While he was gone, the rest of the family had raised the cotton from plowtime to harvest. He planned to help pick the cotton and to spend the winter preparing new ground. Then it was back to Texas for good.

Reluctant to proceed, he stood in the sparse shade of the scraggly trees wishing he had a choice. At twenty-one, he knew he was full-grown. More than six months of being on his own had made him independent. Well, almost on his own, he conceded mentally—working for Uncle Prent, eating at Aunt Betty's table, bunking with their boys. But they treated him like a man—never asking him where he had been when he stayed out all night, just expecting a full day's hard work the next day same as any other hired hand. He half expected his family to treat him like a child again.

Even as he hesitated he felt a pull toward the family he had not seen in several months. Spotting an ironing board supported on the top rungs of two ladder-back chairs under one of the trees, he wondered which of his sisters had set it up to escape the stifling heat inside the house. As he watched, the front screen door banged open and his sister Flora appeared testing a hot iron with the wet forefinger of her left hand. He chuckled when she jerked the finger away without touching the iron.

The team had been quiet since they stopped, but suddenly both horses blew at once. Flora raised her head at the sound, stared a moment, then started running toward them.

"*Ma.* Ma, here's Ben," she flung toward the house as she ran.

Ben flicked the horses with the lines and descended the low grade. He had reached the yard when his mother rushed out of the house drying her hands on her apron. Flora seemed to realize she had a hot iron in her hand and returned inside to set it on the stove.

Ben jumped down and picked up his frail mother in his arms. She felt smaller than he remembered. He said, "Ma, you're no bigger than a piece of soap after a hard day's washing." She clung to him, crying.

Seeing Flora approaching, Ben set his mother down. As he watched his mother dry her eyes on a corner of her apron, Ben pinched the moisture from his eyes with his thumb and finger and wished he had a clean handkerchief.

Flora stood with hands clasped behind her back, bare feet squirming in the red dirt. Ben noticed how womanly she had become. Her body had developed early, but now at seventeen she looked grown up. Her dark brown hair smoothed into a knot at the nape of her neck marked her transition from pigtailed childhood. There was an air of confidence about her that belied the shyness that she exhibited. He held out his arms to his favorite sister and she ran into them.

Flora sobbed and clung to him. He held her head against his shoulder and let her cry. Over her head he exchanged glances with his mother and decided Ma was deeply worried about something. Was she worried about Flora?

"I'm sure glad to see you, Son," his mother said.

Ben and Flora had always been close, closer than Jed and Flora although they were right next to each other. He recollected the night of Flora's birth. Pa had taken Buford and Paul to Uncle Prent's when he went after Aunt Betty to be with Ma. But he and Jed had already gone to bed and his parents decided they were too little to notice anything.

Ma said, "After all, Matt, this is my sixth one and I know I won't carry on like some women. I've been through it enough to know how I'll act. I don't think the little ones will even wake up."

Ben had scrooched up his eyes real tight so they would think he was asleep. Important events he surely didn't want to miss must be about to happen. He had tried his little-boy best to stay awake but he hadn't even known when Pa came back with Aunt Betty and Mrs. Taylor, the midwife. At daylight he opened his eyes to see Pa standing by his bed, saying, "Ben, you have a baby sister."

Ben raised up on one elbow when Pa laid the little baby down next to him. His four-year-old heart came right up in his throat as he felt the warmth from the tiny bundle. With a trembling hand, he pulled the blanket corner away from her face and looked at her tight-shut eyes and shock of pale hair. As he rubbed one finger gently against her cheek, awe filled his body from head to toe as he felt its downy softness.

Pa said, "Ben, would you like to name her?"

Ben had an old rag doll named Flora that he loved so much that he played with her even though his older brothers teased him until he cried. He said, "Pa, can we name her Flora?"

He realized when he was older that his parents had picked the name first and guessed he would name the baby Flora. But by that time, it hadn't mattered. Flora had always been *his* sister.

Arms around his knees on one side and another pair around his chest from behind him announced the arrival of his little brother and sister. He had heard them shouting as they came up behind him and had let Flora go. He scooped Betsy up and whirled to hug Holt. "I swear, y'all are getting so big I can't hold you both at once."

Betsy giggled and Holt chuckled. He swung Betsy to his shoulders, carried her to a bed that had been moved to the yard, and dropped her sprawling upon it. She scrambled up and held out her arms to him.

"Nope, not now, Little Bit. I have to take care of the team. Come on, Holt, you help me."

"Ben I'm so glad you're here," Ma said. "We sure been needing you, Son."

After Ben finished with the horses and washed up, his mother filled a plate with garden vegetables and cornbread for him. She poured a tall glass of buttermilk and set it beside the plate as he sat down at the table, then shooed the young ones outside. "Go back to your play and let Ben eat in peace. Go on now, you won't have a chance to play until the cotton is in, now that Ben's here with the other wagon. We'll fill one wagon and send it to the gin while we fill the other."

As he ate, his mother stood at the wood stove beating a mixture in the top of a double boiler. She kept glancing at the antique kitchen clock while concentrating on the job at hand.

Ben relaxed somewhat as the good food filled his stomach and the quiet minutes ticked by. He watched his mother lift the pan of icing from the water, add vanilla, and pour half of it into a skillet, stirring as she did so.

Then she moved to the table and began to ice a white two-layer cake with the frosting. "I hope that burnt sugar icing turns out all right," she said. "I don't usually make a double recipe, but I wanted to make a Brownstone Front cake with burnt sugar icing for Flora. She doesn't know I'm making it for her. She thinks I made the two cakes for the party tonight, one for Ida and the other for Polly."

Reluctantly, Ben asked the question that had been pestering him. Here he was, plunk in the middle of family problems when he had promised himself to hold aloof. But he couldn't ignore it if something bothered Flora. "Ma, what was Flora crying about?"

Lillie finished the white cake and poured the other frosting into the top of the double boiler before she answered. Setting the pan into the boiling water on the stove, she muttered, "I hope I can save this," and attacked the mixture with the beater again. Finally satisfied that the icing had reached spreading stage, she sat at the table to ice the other cake.

Knowing his mother's nature to take her own good time, Ben had waited patiently. I'm a lot like her, he thought. However, when she appeared to have forgotten him, he prodded her by clearing his throat.

Lillie looked up briefly and returned to her work. "I don't think it's anything serious, just a lot of little things piled up. You know yesterday was her birthday and nobody seemed to pay any extra attention. We had to get the cotton picked so your Pa and Jed could take it to the gin today, and I didn't have time to even bake her a cake. That's the reason I'm making her favorite now. And your Pa's going to pick up coats for each of the girls in town today. We ordered them from the catalog. But you know it's not the same as having things right on your birthday."

She paused to beat the icing a few more strokes. Satisfied with it once again, she began spreading it on the sides of the cake.

Her deliberateness nettled Ben. "Ma, I don't think she'd take it so hard if that was all."

"Well, then today is Ida's birthday, and suddenly everyone's celebrating it. Polly is having a party and I let Ida go over there to spend the day and Flora had to finish Ida's chores. To top it all off, I let Ida wear Flora's new divided skirt. It took her a whole lot of wheedling to get Matt's permission to even have a divided skirt. Then she bought the material with her own money and just finished making the fool thing. She hasn't even got to wear it yet."

Lillie stood and surveyed the two cakes with pleasure. She said, "Ben, you bring the white cake and I'll take this one. We'll put them in the bay window to cool." With the cakes safely cooling, she began washing up the pans and resumed her narrative. Her eyes filled with tears and her voice tightened. "I ought not to've done it, but Ida put the skirt on while Flora and Plez were outside. I knew Ida would be riding behind Paul and, with Plez along, I was afraid she would accidentally expose herself."

It wouldn't be an accident, Ben thought.

CHAPTER 2

Paul

Early that same morning, Paul Conover had watched for a chance to talk privately with his father. Jed and Ida had finished milking when Flora called them for breakfast. Paul pretended to be having trouble with the harness until they were out of earshot.

"Pa," he called, "can I talk to you a minute?"

Matt Conover stopped in the barn doorway and looked back.

"Pa, you know Buford didn't come home last night."

"Well, that's not too unusual, Paul. He probably got in a poker game and played all night."

"No, Pa." His throat constricted and he found it hard to breathe. When he had rehearsed this conversation in his mind, he had thought it would be easy to tell his father. After all, he reasoned Pa had been a Texas Ranger and he must recognize Paul's ambition to be a lawman. He had only been doing a little detective work.

Matt cleared his throat, a sure sign he was getting impatient. "Well, Pa, it was like this. I had started to town and I just happened to go by Sid Drumm's place." Without looking at his father, Paul decided not to explain how he happened to go by the Drumm farm on the way to town. Pa knew it lay in the opposite direction. He hurried on, "It was just after dark and I heard a commotion. There wasn't anyone home at Drumm's place, looked like, so I decided I'd better take a look. I tied Old Spot to that dead tree there by the creek and slipped up to the barn."

The way Pa tensed and held himself so stiff and quiet stilled Paul's hesitant accounting of his actions of the previous night. The breathing of the horses and the morning calls of waking birds sounded deafening to him. Cautiously he peered through his eyelashes at his father. The scowl on Matt's face made Paul remember black clouds and storms. All at once, the detective work seemed more like spying. Matt waited unmoving and Paul knew he had to finish his story.

"Th-there were three men driving off all of S-Sid's horses." He stopped and took a few deep breaths. When he continued, he talked slowly to control his stutter. "Pa, I swear it was Buford and the Sexton boys. I didn't let them know I was anywhere around. I hate to admit it, but I was scared, I guess."

Matt seemed to be thinking of something else. Paul spoke louder. "Pa, what should I do?"

"Do, Paul? Do? About what?"

"Pa, haven't you been listening? I said I saw Buford stealing horses. *Stealing horses*, Pa. I know he has always been a little wild, but now that he's running with the Sexton boys he has turned into a thief. A *thief*, Pa."

Even though he could not see his father's face in shadow against the dawning light, Paul knew it exhibited Matt's most flinty expression. His voice pitched higher and he had trouble managing his stutter. "Pa, you know I always wanted to be a Ranger like you. When they wouldn't take me, all I could th-think about was moving to a new country where they're going to need lawmen more than they do at home. I just couldn't think about anything else. So I started hounding you to come up here. I've never told you this, Pa, but I always had to be just like you. I *had* to. I had to show you I was as good as Ben. You were always so partial to Ben, letting him do everything."

Paul paused and raised his head. He had been unable to look directly at his father while speaking of his deep feelings. He couldn't understand why Pa still said nothing. He clinched his hands into fists to lessen their trembling and to steady his shaking voice.

"Well, anyway, Pa, I thought if I could catch the Sexton boys, it would show folks up here that I could make them a good lawman even if I am just going on twenty-four. Everybody knows who's been doing all the meanness around here. But, Pa, it's different with Buford mixed up in it. I don't know what to do. If it wasn't for you and Ma, I'd go ahead and turn them all in."

When Matt still didn't answer, Paul rushed on. "Pa, he makes me so m-mad, doing this to you. You have always been so g-good. So I'm asking you to tell me what to do."

Finally his passion seemed to penetrate his father's silence. But Matt's reply skirted Paul's question.

"Son," he said, "I never was partial to Ben. I love all my children, each one in his own special way. You may think I favored Ben because I let him out of a lot of work. Son, Ben always could do more with your Ma when she had one of her spells than anyone else, even me. That was why I let him stay with her instead of going to the field with the rest of the family. That was why, Paul, not that I was partial to him."

Then he changed the subject. "Son, you know I don't have any spare time this morning. I have to get this load of cotton to the gin and try to get back before dark. We'll have to lay off harvesting today while I'm gone. I was hoping Ben would get here with the other wagon so we could load one while we took the other one to the gin." He turned on his heel and started out the door.

Paul hurried to catch up with him. "But, Pa—"

"We'll talk about it tonight when I get home."

After breakfast, Matt and Jed left with the load of cotton to be ginned. Paul's conflicting emotions chased thoughts around in his head. *If I turn Buford in, it will kill Ma. On the other hand, if I don't,* what kind of lawman can I ever be? Why didn't Pa tell me what to do? No, I'm a grown man; I can make up my own mind. Buford is my big brother. How can I ruin him and the family's reputation? He ruined himself. If he will go to the sheriff and testify against the Sextons, it will go easier on him. I'll find Buford and talk to him about it.

Decision made, Paul hurried to finish the chores so he would have more time to hunt Buford and present his proposal. He led his saddled horse out of the barn just as Plez Wilson rode up. Plez lived with his family a mile west of the Conover farm. A year younger than Paul, he was a square-built man with straight black hair and laughing brown eyes. His always-smiling mouth and sharp dry humor drew attention away from his big nose and ears. Half-Choctaw on his mother's side, Plez inherited her reddish-brown complexion.

He reined his horse and called to Paul, "Can y'all come to a dance at our house tonight?"

"You bet." Paul ambled over to the visitor. "You just starting to round everybody up?"

"Yeah, I've been to the McMasters' already and Uncle Stump's. If you're not busy, come go with me."

Paul hesitated. "I've got something to do later. How long do you figure you'll be?"

"Be through by noon, I reckon. Come on."

"Sure, let me tell Ma where I'm going."

Plez slid down from his horse. "I've got to see your Ma anyhow. Today is Ida's birthday, too, isn't it? Polly wants me to see if Ida can come to our house and stay until tonight. We can go back that way with her as far as Uncle Stump's house. Reckon she'll be okay from there."

Horses tethered to the front porch posts, the two friends crossed the porch laughing and talking. Paul reached for the screen door handle just as Ida appeared on the inside of the door. At fifteen, she had grown tall but had barely begun to fill out. Skinny arms and legs emphasized her height. She straightened her slouched shoulders when she saw Plez, smiled and pranced outside.

He laughed and said, "Well, if it isn't the birthday girl. You think you're big enough to go spend the day with your twin?"

Her eyes glowed and she ran back into the house shouting, "Ma, Ma, can I go spend the day with Polly?"

The men followed and Plez said to their mother, "There's more to it than that. Polly begged until Pa said she could have a dance tonight to celebrate her birthday. Because it's Ida's birthday, too, she wants Ida to come spend the day with her."

Paul said, "I'm going with Plez to invite the neighbors. We'll see she gets there all right."

Flora entered from a back room, closing the door quietly behind her. Paul saw Plez become motionless. Only his eyes moved following her every step. She said to her mother, "Ma, if we're going to a party, we need to do up our clothes. Can Paul draw the water before he goes?"

Plez stepped forward. "I'll draw the water, Missus Conover, if Flora can show me where the tubs are."

Ida jumped ahead of Flora leading the way to the door. Her mother called her back. "You better get ready to go. Flora can help Plez."

Paul went with them to the end of the porch. "Plez, just whistle when you get the tubs full and I'll come help you carry them back." He watched Plez hoist one empty tub to his shoulder and the two of them lift the other tub between them. There goes one happy man, he thought, and wondered how far their relationship could possibly go. Pa is so set against Indians that he won't let Flora walk out with Plez. He goes to church and sits in the row behind her and manages to walk outside with her but, as far as I know, that's as far as it goes.

Once the two men had dropped Ida at the corner a half-mile from her friend's house, they proceeded throughout the morning riding from house to house inviting all the neighbors. As they cut cross-country, Paul kept a sharp lookout for any trace of his brother or the Sextons. No sign of them or the horses appeared although he searched carefully.

At noon the young men stopped at Plez Wilson's to find the two girls so engrossed in birthday party plans they hadn't prepared a noon meal. Plez seemed embarrassed. His ruddy color deepened as he said, "Polly, get in there and rustle up some grub for us. We didn't get around to all the neighbors this morning and we need to get back on the trail."

Polly hurried to the kitchen but Ida squirmed in her chair and settled herself more solidly.

Paul chided her, "Get up from there and go help her."

She stuck her tongue out at him. "Smarty, we didn't know you'd be here for dinner. We ate cold biscuits and butter and jelly. That's good enough for you, too."

Her brother reached for her, but she evaded him and flounced into the kitchen. Soon the girls called them to the table to a cold meal of sliced ham, potato salad, tomatoes, onions, and cucumber pickles. Since Mrs. Wilson's death two years before, Polly had grown to be a good cook and housekeeper.

Paul saw a great difference in the two girls who celebrated their fifteenth birthday that day. Polly's gentle demeanor belied her tender years while Ida's flipperty nature betrayed rebellion. He had no doubt competent Polly could handle preparations for the celebration tonight if Ida didn't distract her. He wondered at the close friendship of the two with such different dispositions.

In the afternoon the men rode to the homes between the Wilson place and town but did not go into the town itself. Mr. Wilson had agreed to spread the word from his general store.

When they parted, Plez said, "Pa's going to let his clerk close the store tonight so he can come home early and bring ice for the ice cream. We've borrowed an extra freezer from the neighbors and I could use a little help. Come early and help me chip ice and start freezing the cream."

Paul promised with a nod of his head, his mind absorbed by logistics of hunting for Buford and the horses. All morning, he had studied the woodland for signs on the ground or in the brush: a broken limb, scuffed bark, trampled undergrowth and scattered leaves, or footprints. Near Sid Drumm's property, no telltale evidence could he see. They must have led the animals down the well-traveled road in the dark. He had been unable to search for marks the men or horses left when they entered the road from Drumm's property because Plez had insisted on cutting through the woods a quarter mile from Drumm's.

Saluting Plez with a hand to his hat, he parted from him and cut cross-country toward the Drumm place intending to follow the road from their point of departure of the morning. He kept a lookout for any indication that the stolen horses had traveled through the area even though he did not expect to find any clues there.

By concentrating ahead of time on tracks and listening to sounds of nature, he expected to sharpen his focus when he needed it. But he found it hard to keep his mind from returning to the sweet face of Polly Wilson as she served her guests. His hand itched to stroke her heavy hair that was black as a crow's feathers. He smelled in retrospect her clean, starched dress and the faint woodsy scent of her skin. Her eyes almost as black as her hair had returned his gaze without blinking.

Until today he had always thought her shy because she talked little. But when her hand touched his as she passed the biscuits, she hadn't jerked it away. She had folded her lips slightly in a secret little smile. A man could do much worse than have her to wife.

The horse pulled hard against his slack hand and Paul saw they had reached the new road leading into their homestead. He urged the horse on down the main road until after they passed the track he and Ben had hacked out last winter. Not wanting to be seen around

Sid Drumm's place that lay across the road a half mile ahead, he guided the horse off the road to skirt the property and approached from the shallow creek that ran behind it.

Nearing the Drumm house, Paul heard a woman's high-pitched outcry, "Git outta here now. Go on, git."

With the horses hooves muffled in the dry sandy creek bottom, he felt safe from discovery as he rode close enough to see the cause of the commotion. He saw Mrs. Drumm stoop to pick up a rock and throw it at a black and white dog that had its nose to the ground at the gate of the corral. Absorbed in the scent, the animal paid no attention to the woman until the third rock found its mark. It yelped and turned to see the source of the attack. Intent on keeping his presence secret, Paul had kept his attention focused on the woman, but the dog's howl drew his gaze to the dog. Immediately recognizing Old Bob, he whistled.

If Mrs. Drumm heard the low note, she gave no indication. Her attention directed at the dog, she bent to pick up another rock.

Paul whistled again and Bob sped toward him, tail wagging excitedly. Turning the horse, Paul retraced his path until he was certain that he was out of sight and earshot of the house.

Back in Texas, Paul had often hunted with Old Bob while riding Spot and the horse plodded along paying no mind to the dog that bounced around them. Paul talked to the dog as they moved along. "So good, sweet Ben brought you with him, huh? Stole Uncle Prent's favorite pup, huh? Where is Ben, anyway?"

Despite his jealously of his brother, Paul considered returning home and leaving his quest until another day. He had to admit he respected Ben's judgment. Maybe he should talk his problem over with Ben and get his opinion.

But the sun still rode high. Another couple of hours hunting time remained before he needed to go help Plez with the ice cream. Now that he had Bob with him, he could try to bag a few squirrels. He always carried his rifle with him. It made a good excuse to be cutting through the countryside. Not that he needed an excuse. It was not an activity that anyone questioned.

First he followed the route he had laid out in his mind earlier in the day, circling the Drumm property to observe any sign of the trail the thieves had followed. When he found no trace of their path, he felt sure of his suspicion that they had used the main road.

Any vestige of hoof marks had long since been erased by traffic into town. Cotton farmers had begun taking their first pickings to the gin. Although school had been delayed until after October first by the Chickasaw school board, the white settlers in town were working to form their own training establishment, going from house to house to recruit students. Truly traffic had picked up as settlers flocked to the Territory which was in a transition period to become the forty-sixth state.

Paul reluctantly reached the conclusion that his planned pursuit had ended in frustration. He might as well follow the dog to see if he treed a squirrel or two.

True to his natural instinct, Bob soon found game, and in a short while Paul had three young squirrels tied to his saddle. He called the dog to head home, but Bob did not mind him. He had his nose to the ground and took off without looking back.

Paul whistled and called to no avail. "You're cold-trailing, boy," he said. Nevertheless, he found no alternative but to follow along.

Soon they entered a heavily wooded area Paul had never seen. He marked the position of the sun and spotted landmarks to guide him back home. Then he began seeing evidence of recent activity: tree limbs broken, scuffed leaves, horse hair snagged in bark. Bob's following Buford's scent, he thought.

Paul eased down from his horse and tied him to a tree. He walked with care, making no sound. Bob had disappeared but Paul had no problem following. Sign of recent activity abounded. Apparently the men had expended no effort to cover their trail here.

Careful not to be seen, Paul eased forward. Still sheltered by heavy woods, he saw ahead of him a clearing fenced in one corner with post and rail. Horses milled around inside the fence and Paul estimated their number at more than twenty. Shocked, he realized the extent of planning and effort employed in the operation.

At the corner of the corral, Bob sat with his head on Buford's knee. Buford knelt rubbing the old dog's head. Paul had forgotten the close relationship the man and dog had forged when Buford worked for Uncle Prent in Texas. Ever since first finding Buford's scent, Bob had hunted until he found him. I'd never have looked in this area without Bob, Paul told himself.

Only a minute or two had passed when Buford stood and called, "Come on in, Paul. I'm by myself."

Paul advanced cautiously. "How'd you know it was me?"

Buford snorted. "You're lucky I'm minding the hideout instead of Camp and Al, especially Al. In fact, you're doubly lucky because one of them was supposed to relieve me before now. I'm warning you, you'd better hie yourself away from here as fast as you can. Don't let them catch you or you'll regret it."

Undeterred, Paul hastily pursued the strategy he had worked out that morning. "Buford, you know I've got to stop this thievery. The Sexton boys—I don't mind turning them in. Truth, it will give me pleasure. But I can't just tattle on you, so I'm asking you to go to the sheriff yourself. You know, if you testify against the Sextons, it will go better on you."

Buford's look of cold contempt chilled Paul to the bone. "P-please, Brother, I'm begging you. Think what this will do to Ma."

"You think it will be any easier on Ma if you turn me in? Now, go on. Get out of here."

Paul tried once more. "Buford, come with me—"

But Buford cut him off. "You're not listening. I've warned you to leave. Now you'd better skedaddle before my relief gets here. It's bad enough now. I'll have to explain the dog. You know he'll stay with me."

Turning on his heel, Paul retraced his steps toward his horse. Back stiff, he tried not to betray his emotions, but he could not contain. He turned and in a broken voice said once again, "Please, Buford."

When he received no response, he mounted, made his rifle secure, and making no effort to be quiet, rode away.

CHAPTER 3

Matt

If there was one driving force in Matt Conover's life, it centered on his wife, Lillie. As he guided the team onto the main road to begin his trip to the cotton gin in Healdton, he forced his thoughts away from his troubles with his oldest son. With an effort of will, he deliberately turned them to his first meeting with the dark-haired beauty who had been the light and the darkness of his life for twenty-seven years come December.

In that January of 1879, unsettled in his mind about his future, he had signed on for a second enlistment with the Texas Rangers. At twenty-nine, unmarried and at loose ends because of the death of his widowed mother whose constant care had been his responsibility for three years, it had seemed a way to make a little money while he considered his prospects. He knew most of the men in the company having served with them in the Indian uprising of seventy-three and, in that sparsely settled county, their duties left them plenty of time to complete their farm chores and raise a crop.

His tour had hardly begun when the captain took him on an assignment to notify a family of the death of their son. "You need to learn how to tell bad news," Captain O'Neill told him. The task had become more complicated when they learned the deceased had a wife living in the next county. Rather than send word to the Rangers in that county, the captain had decided to send Matt to break the news.

With mixed feelings of trepidation and a growing assurance that he was equal to the task, young Matt took the three-day journey. He had found the farmhouse after an inquiry or two and soon rode into the clean-swept yard. Dried sheets snapped on a clothesline in the West Texas wind and, battling to hold them away from the dirt while she unpinned them was a little girl he judged to be about twelve years old. She was of slight build and, when gusts of wind jerked the sheets, her feet lifted off the ground.

Matt sprang from his horse and ran to help her. Glad to have his assistance, she pulled the pins from the line while he gathered up the linens. Laughing, she led him to the house and invited him in.

Remembering his sad duties, he shook his head and asked, "Is your mother home?"

He knew he would never forget her peal of musical laughter as she said, "I'm the mother in this house."

Matt looked at her more carefully. Black, curly hair caught up in a red ribbon on the back of her head fell in a cascade almost to her waist. Her diminutive size had fooled him into thinking her to be little more than a child. On closer inspection, he saw something in her face and bearing that marked her as an adult although, if pressed, he knew he could not define that something. This woman looked as if she could handle the news he had brought her if, indeed, she turned out to be the widow.

Brought back to the present by a sudden jolt of the spring seat, he turned to see Jed settle on the seat beside him. Jed had climbed atop the cotton, sleepyhead as usual, and had fallen asleep instantly. Surprised at his taking such a short nap, Matt asked, "What's the matter?"

"I felt every seed every time I moved. Want to give me the lines? What did you do while I was dozing?"

Matt smiled. This son wanted everyone to account for every minute. "I slapped at flies with the lines and held the horses on the road and—"

Jed cut him off. "I know you, you were making plans to get more work out of me."

Matt wished he could tell Jed his worry about Buford. When he told Paul that he loved each one of his children in a different way, he meant it. And he knew each one through and through. Although Jed was his favorite for companionship, he possessed little judgment. Of course, at nineteen years of age, he still had a lot of maturing to do. He said, "I was thinking of the day I met your mother."

"I've heard that story a hundred times," Jed said. "What I don't know much about is my half-brother. You never talk about him."

"There's no reason not to talk about him, Jed, except it hurts your Ma so much even after all these years that I never bring it up and she never does, either. When he died was when she had her first spell."

"Tell me all about him. I won't say a word to Ma."

Oh, yes, you will, Matt thought. You can't help it.

"The first time I saw Terence was the day I came to bring your Ma the tidings of the death of the sorry excuse for a man who sired him. I can't call that man his Pa. I was little Terence's Pa for half his life, and the other half, he had no Pa as far as I'm concerned."

In his mind's eye, he saw again the frail child as he had seen him that day when he followed Lillie into the house. She had gone into the kitchen to fetch coffee while he walked around the front room looking at pictures and bric-a-brac. The little boy stood shyly at the end of a china cabinet thinking to be hidden by it.

Matt had smiled at the boy and sat down within sight of him. Absently, he twirled the watch fob hanging from his pant's pocket. Overcome with curiosity, Terence ventured closer to him, but did not come near enough to touch.

Matt removed the watch from his pocket, looked at the time, and started to put it back in his pocket. Then, as if noticing the child for the first time, he smiled again and held the watch toward him.

When Lillie returned with the coffee, Terence had been leaning against Matt's knee, listening to the ticking of the watch while Matt held it to his ear.

Lillie said, "I've not seen him take up with a stranger that quickly before. How did you manage that?"

He paused in his narration when Jed pulled the horses to a stop while he checked for traffic at a corner. "Pa, why are we going to Healdton instead of Chagris? It's farther from the farm."

"I heard the gin there pays thirteen cents. Even a copper more a pound means a lot these days," Matt told him.

Jed turned left toward Healdton, and said, "Go on with your story, Pa."

I'll skip the part about telling Lillie about her husband, Matt thought. That's her story to tell if she wants to.

"Terence was a sickly child. He had been mistreated and hurt somewhere inside when he was a tiny baby, and he never got over it. But he and I hit it off the first time we saw each other. I reckon that was one reason your Ma didn't run me off. She protected all her children, but she was fierce as a she-bear shielding Terence from any hurt. And, of course, I was, too.

"He could walk and move around all right, but he couldn't run and play. When Buford was born, and later Paul, you could tell he wished he had the strength, but he never complained. And the boys were good to him, but they were just children."

Jed's attention seemed to wander and Matt questioned whether he should continue, but Jed said, "Tell me about when he died. That was before I was born."

"Yes, Lillie was pregnant with Ben, about eight months along. It was winter and we thought Terence had taken a little cold. But it turned into pneumonia. He was too frail to overcome it. Both the other boys got sick, too—not bad like Terence—and Lillie and I both were up night and day nursing the three of them.

"Then Terence died." He shook his head in disbelief at the memory. "It was a bad time, I tell you. I don't know how we got through it. We did, finally, but not very well. I think Buford and Paul were affected more than most people realize." Mentioning Buford and Paul brought his troubles of the present to mind. With an effort he refused to think of them just now and continued, "but I'm getting ahead of my story.

"We buried him in the family cemetery next to his grandmother Holt. Buford and Paul were recovering by that time, sleeping all night. It was a good thing, too, because Lillie went into labor early and Ben was born prematurely. You know it is harder to save an eight-month baby than a seven-month. I don't know why. Lillie thought she would lose another son and she just went out of her head. It lasted for months. Her sisters took turns staying and looking after the children. I'll always be grateful to them for that, neglecting their families for ours.

"Finally, it was Ben who brought her out of it. At first, we were afraid to leave her alone with him. Then we noticed that she seemed calm and at peace as she took care of him. He had gained weight and she took pleasure in feeding him. She carried him with her to Terence's grave where she spent hours. When she worked on the grave, she laid him on a pallet beside her. More time each day she was at herself and finally she became her old self again."

Matt realized Jed had said nothing for a time. He stopped his narrative and looked closely at his son. Jed seemed lost in deep thought, his brow wrinkled and his eyes unseeing.

"Something bothering you, Son?"

Jed shook his head as if he had just awakened. He blinked at his father and appeared to consider his question for several minutes while the clop-clop of the horse's hooves kept time with the rattling of the wagon.

Matt waited, surprised that Jed had not replied quickly, as was his nature.

Finally, Jed said, "No, Pa. I've got some things on my mind, but I'll have to work them out myself."

Matt probed gently, "Everything all right between you and Essie?"

Jed's eyes lighted with the thought of his sweetheart, but his expression remained somber. "All's well in that quarter. Yes, all's well with Essie."

Matt waited for Jed to ask him to continue his story, but, when his son fell back into a deep reverie, his own thoughts turned to the morning's discussion with Paul. Discussion is not the right word, Matt reflected. I left him hanging but I had to consider how to answer him about Buford. I reckon I did a pretty fair job of keeping the family in the dark about Buford's dealings in Texas if nosy Paul failed to smell it out. Lord knows I wouldn't have left Texas except to keep Buford out of jail. Lillie would never get over that.

He closed one eye and squinted at the sun beginning to burn hot above the eastern horizon. Taking the lines from Jed, he slapped the horses with them and said, "Come on, boys, we've got a ways to go this day. No telling how long we'll have to wait at the gin."

CHAPTER 4

Ben

Ben jumped slightly when his mother stopped talking in the middle of a sentence and glanced over his shoulder toward the front door. He saw Flora struggling with the ironing board and hastened to help her.

Flora had been in and out all afternoon changing the cooled iron for a hot one but had not lingered nor said a word, which was unlike her. Quiet but sociable, she usually exchanged pleasantries each time she encountered another person as she went efficiently about her business.

"We keep the ironing board behind the door in the bedroom," she told Ben. While he went to put it away, she turned to her mother. "I'll get my shoes on and go after the cows. We need to finish the chores early today."

Feeling a need to talk with her privately, Ben said, "I'll go with you. Let me get my hat."

Finding the cattle proved to take only a few minutes. They seemed inclined to keep on grazing and Ben sat on a fallen log and patted it to invite Flora to sit beside him. "We haven't had a chance to talk yet," he said.

Flora sat beside him with head bowed, not saying anything.

"Come on, Flossie," Ben coaxed, using his pet name for her. "This isn't like you. You haven't said two words to me since I got here. Remember me? I'm big brother. Tell me what's troubling you. Ma said this afternoon you cried because of Ida, but I don't believe it for a minute. Come on, Kid, spill it."

Flora raised her head slowly and turned to him with tears spilling down her cheeks. "I haven't told anyone, but I know I can trust you, Ben. The truth is that I'm in love with Plez Wilson, and Pa won't even let me walk out with him. We've had to slip in a chance meeting here and there. We just never get to be alone together." She choked on her tears, put her head in her hands, and sobbed.

"But I don't see why Pa forbids you to talk to him, Flora. I only met him a time or two when I was here before, but he seems a pleasant enough fellow. What's the problem?"

"You don't realize. Plez is Indian, at least his Ma was. Pa is terribly set against white folks and Indians marrying. Then, too, Plez's Uncle Stump is a bootlegger. It's not only against the law, but for an Indian to be one is the very worst thing that can be."

She pulled a handkerchief from her apron pocket, wiped her eyes, and blew her nose. "Ma suspicioned how Plez and I were beginning to feel about each other. He started coming to church with Polly and sitting with her and Ida. Of course, I always sit with Essie McMasters, but they sit right behind us. Anyway, she told Pa her think-so and he called me in privately and said he was going to nip this thing in the bud. He said if you never get to know somebody, it's unlikely you'll marry him. And in case I didn't understand him, he was forbidding me right now to marry Plez Wilson or any Indian."

"So, that's that, then," Ben said. "You can't disobey Pa; none of us can, except Buford. And you can see how much that hurts Pa. It looks like you'll just have to get over it some way. I'll help all I can, but I can't help you go against Pa."

Flora looked at Ben as if he had slapped her. Her eyes blazed and the tears dried. "I thought I could count on *you*. I've been waiting until you got home to have you help me decide what to do, no, to have you help me do what I know I have to do. But you are going to be just like Pa. He says it's all right to try to get along with *them*. After all, we live in their country. But we don't want to mix with *them* too much." She spat out "them" as if she were hearing her father say it to her.

Suddenly, she jumped up and began pacing in the small area, picking up sticks, and flinging them as far as she could throw them. Finally, she stopped in front of Ben, and, dry-eyed, but with trembling voice, said, "When Plez stopped to pick up Paul this morning, he begged me to run off with him and get married. I haven't decided yet what I'll do. But I know now I can't count on you."

With that, she rounded up the cows and started for home. Ben hurried to catch up with them, but the cows knew the way home. Neither he nor Flora had anything to do but walk along silently behind them. It was the first time he could remember that he and Flora had been at cross-purposes and he for certain didn't how to handle it.

CHAPTER 5

Ben

By the time Ben and Flora finished the evening milking, Lillie had prepared herself and the two younger children for the party. She had folded a quilt in quarters and spread it in Ben's wagon, placed large pans containing the birthday cakes on it, and covered them with another quilt.

"I'll take care of the milk while you two get ready. We need to get going."

"Ma," Holt said, "I'm going to start out walking. I can cut through and I bet I'll beat you there." He ran out the door with Betsy right behind him. He whirled and ran back. "Ma, make her go with you. She'll just slow me down."

Lillie gave Betsy a look that said, Stay. Betsy let out a howl and stomped her foot. Holt had already disappeared.

Lillie tipped the bucket to drain the last few drops of milk through the strainer. Then, she set about rinsing the milk pails, strainer, and strainer cloth in cold water before washing and scalding them. Betsy had dried her eyes by the time her mother completed the job.

Ben appeared in the doorway after cleaning up in the dugout and Flora came in from her bedroom about the same time.

"I hitched the team, Ma. We're ready to go."

When they arrived at the Wilson place, Holt had indeed beaten them there. Still panting from his run, he greeted them triumphantly. "See there, I told you I'd get here first."

Betsy hit him and ran. He started chasing her.

Lillie let them go. "Come on," she said to Flora. "I know the girls can use our help. You carry this pan and I'll get the other. Ben, I think you should hunt up Plez and help him."

Ben found Plez, whom he remembered from the winter before, in the shade of the house turning the crank on a large ice cream freezer.

Plez stood to shake hands when Ben asked what he could do to help. Plez indicated his chair and said, "You crank. I'll chip more ice." As Ben spun the handle, Plez added ice and salt alternately.

"You've just started on this freezer, haven't you? It's too easy to turn."

An exasperated scowl crossed Plez's face. "Yeah, your brother, Paul, promised to come early and I waited for him thinking it wouldn't take long to make two freezers with us both working at it. I finally started, but this is the first freezer full. I wonder what happened to him."

"He didn't come home, for sure. Ma expected him back to do the evening chores. She said she didn't know what she would have done if I hadn't come home. Pa and Jed went to Healdton with a load of cotton and we know they'll be late getting in."

Plez finished filling the ice and salt, mounded it over the top of the freezer, and placed two folded tow sacks over it. "I'll go see if Polly has the other freezer ready. We borrowed another gallon-and-a-half freezer from McMasters."

He walked two hesitant steps, stopped and turned to look at Ben. "What do you suppose happened to him?"

"I can't imagine," Ben said. "He's usually the most dependable one of us. I bet when he shows up he'll have some story to tell."

However, they had seen no sign of Paul an hour later when the house and yard filled with guests. Plez introduced Ben to the men as they arrived. Ben knew he had met many of them before and he repeated "Your face is familiar but I can't recollect your name" over and over.

When the McMasters family drove in and the men carried their musical instruments into the house, most of the men who had been standing around outside followed them to start the dancing. Ben remembered meeting the McMasters boys at other dances, but he had not seen their parents or their sisters on his earlier trip.

As he hung back behind the group to finish the cigarette he had just rolled, he saw a group of men gathered around a wagon and observed Stump McIntosh selling them jars of moonshine. Dryness clutched his throat and he felt the familiar tightness in his stomach that unfamiliar situations always prompted. He took a long drag on the cigarette as he turned toward the wagon. Hesitating on the bottom step, he pictured his mother's expression if she smelled whiskey on his breath. Up to now he had hidden his indulgence from her. He felt certain Pa knew even though he had said nothing to him about it, but Ben's imagination envisioned vivid scenes if Matt suspected one of his children caused their mother any pain. He dropped the cigarette stub in the dirt and ground it out with his boot before he turned to go into the house.

The Wilson house, built in a design similar to many in the southwestern area, featured two rooms that sat one behind the other with a porch surrounding them on three sides. The rest of the house was the same width as the porch and front room area combined. Seven doors opened off the porch, three into the front room, two into the next room, and one into a room behind the porch on each side. Ben chose the door nearest him and entered the dining room. He saw only one piece of furniture in the room—a walnut sideboard—because the room had been cleared for dancing. Through a door into the kitchen he could see the dining table laden with serving plates, glasses, cups and silverware. Apparently some of the dining chairs had been moved into the front room while others had been pushed out onto the porch.

Clusters of people dotted the room, separated according to gender. Some men leaned against walls while others stood turned halfway toward them pretending not to be interested in the groups of chattering and laughing girls. The door opposite Ben opened to admit a new family of arrivals and all turned to welcome them. Ben took the opportunity to ease his way to the door opening into the front room.

This room, too, had been cleared for dancing by pushing all the furniture against the walls. The McMasters brothers had positioned dining chairs near the upright piano and laid out their instruments—fiddles, guitars and a five-string banjo. Their youngest sister tapped keys on the piano as they plucked the stringed instruments, each man laying down a tuned instrument and picking up another until they seemed satisfied. He tried to connect the names of the three brothers with their faces, and finally succeeded in identifying the leader as Horace when he spoke quietly to his sister to begin the first number.

After playing a few bars, Claude, the oldest brother, stood and removed the fiddle from under his chin and cradled it in his left arm. "Choose your partners," he called loudly. Sounds of shuffling feet, slamming doors, and excited laughter filled the two rooms as four couples quickly formed a square in each room. The quartet launched into a lively hoedown while Claude called the moves or tucked the fiddle under his chin while the dancers completed a promenade.

Ben had moved out of the doorway and leaned against the wall watching the dancers in the dining room. He saw his sister Flora step out of the kitchen talking over her shoulder to the girl following her. It was the first time he had seen Esther McMasters fully and he felt his breath catch in his throat.

Diminutive although not as small as his mother, she carried her body upright as if to stretch an extra inch in height. Black wavy hair caught in a green satin ribbon at the nape of her neck framed a face with skin so white as to seem waxy. However the effect was one not of pallor but instead of fine china. He could not see the color of her eyes at this distance but the lashes framing them and the straight brows were as black as her hair. He spied a gleam in her eyes as her full lips turned upward in a quick, impish grin. She leaned forward to whisper to Flora and as she did she swept the room with her glance. Not wanting to be caught staring, Ben dropped his own gaze to her feet, then slowly raised his head. Her full white dress made of some filmy material featured a wide green ribbon sash that matched the one in her hair. He had never seen such a small waist and understood the definition of hourglass figure for the first time.

When his survey reached her face again, she was looking straight at him. Their eyes held for a moment and he felt his heart beat faster. The two girls started his way and he waited for the introduction. But Flora steered Esther through the door into the front room. She's still mad at me, he thought, and felt tension in all his muscles as frustration gripped him. He waited a few minutes and followed, but found that the girls had joined a group of young women watching the quadrille in the center of the room. Slipping through a side door, he stationed himself on the dim porch at the point affording the best view of Esther. When the set ended, partners chose all of the girls in the group except Esther for the next round. He saw Flora and Plez take their place in line for a reel.

Esther appeared unchanged by being passed over, watched the dancers for a few minutes, and then made her way into the dining room out of his sight. He pinched out the cigarette he had just lighted and put it in his pocket. One of the young men he had met earlier opened the door of the dining room and Ben followed him in. Esther stood near the doorway of the front room talking with two girls. Ben edged his way around the wall until he was behind them facing the kitchen door. He could see his mother rearranging the serving table to place another cake brought by one of the women who had just arrived. The women had taken over the kitchen and he saw Ida and Polly dancing in this set.

Trying not to seem forward, he still managed to find a spot behind Esther where he could observe her. She looked back at him, smiled, and then resumed her conversation with the girls.

Guests continued to arrive as daylight deepened into evening. Ben saw the outside door of the kitchen open and his brother Jed's head appear. Jed looked around before he entered holding a large box behind him as if to hide it. He handed it to their mother who set it behind the wood box. Jed proceeded to the dining room door and Ben saw his face light up as he hurried into the room. Certain that Jed had seen him, Ben grinned back. But Jed stopped when he reached Esther who had taken a step forward to meet him. He didn't even see me, Ben thought.

Ben cleared his throat. Jed looked toward him and grinned as he extended his hand. The two men shook hands and then hugged each other with much backslapping, both of them talking at once. The music ended and, in the quiet that followed, Ida joined them and gave Ben a big hug. Esther had not taken part in their greeting and looked awkward. Ida put her arm around Esther and said, "Ben, have you met Jed's sweetheart?" Esther flushed and lowered her eyes. Ida giggled, "Well, you are and everybody knows it." Jed said nothing but took Esther's hand and squeezed it.

Ben felt as if all his strength drained out through his boots. He cast about in his mind for something to say but found only inappropriate words. He wanted to strangle Ida for embarrassing Esther while he felt of two minds about his brother. Why, oh why, had they both fallen for the same girl? Why wasn't he the one who had stayed with the folks and sent Jed back to Texas? He knew the answers but he didn't want a logical explanation, at least not at the moment. He wanted to slink out, crawl in a burrow, and lick his wounds. It didn't matter that no one else seemed aware that he had wounds. He shook his head as if coming out of a fight and realized that the rest of the people in the room had turned to look at the girl standing in the doorway.

Ben could see nothing remarkable about the girl. Her hair was light brown and skinned back in a tight bun on her neck. She wore no makeup while all the other girls had on face powder and a light tinge of rouge. He heard Ida hiss in his ear, "What's she doing here?" and turned to her with eyebrows raised in question. "That's Vinnie Wade. She's not fit for decent company," Ida whispered.

At that moment they heard the ensemble begin a waltz. Distracted, Ida said, "Goody, they're playing a round dance." Couples paired off, holding each other's arms with hands above the other's elbows. Ida asked Jed to dance with her. "Esther believes round dancing is a sin," she explained to Ben.

Jed's face reddened and he clinched his fists. "Ida, some day I'm going to kill you. When are you going to learn to keep your mouth shut?"

Vinnie Wade had approached them. No one in the group spoke to her but she seemed undaunted. "Jed, come dance this one with me," she said. Jed frowned and shook his head. She touched his arm and said, "Please."

Ben felt sorry for her; he decided to ask her to dance with him. It would get him away from his present situation and give him a chance to duck out when the dance was over. But he saw that Jed had changed his mind and walked ahead of her to the edge of the dance area. He took her arms and stood apart from her the customary distance of respect.

Angry at being left standing, Ida flounced out the side door leaving Ben, Flora, and Esther on the edge of the dance floor. Esther whispered to Flora, "My brothers told me to have nothing to do with that girl. She doesn't wear but one petticoat."

Ben overheard the whisper and looked at Flora. Merriment crinkled her eyes. He saw the small muscles around her mouth twitch.

Esther must have seen Flora's mirth because she demanded, "What?"

Flora giggled then. "I wonder how they know."

Ben watched as Esther struggled to hold on to her indignation, but her expression softened and a grin played with her tight lips. A snicker rose to the surface and soon the girls were holding their stomachs as they succumbed to their laughter.

The three of them stood watching the dancers. Ben stepped back behind the two girls to gain an advantage point for observing Esther. He found it hard to overcome his fascination with her. His untenable position became evident to him when she looked only at Jed and Vinnie. Her expression vacillated between disgust and fear. Ben felt like choking his brother for treating Esther in that way even while he exulted that his own attraction for her might have some small chance.

After a few bars Vinnie slid her hands up Jed's arms and moved closer. She leaned forward and whispered in his ear. Jed missed a step and pushed himself away from her. Her expression became more urgent and she seemed to be arguing with Jed. Jed quit dancing and led her out the side door.

Flora gasped and looked at Esther whose face flushed then turned white. Flora took Esther's hand and led her out into the cool night. Ben followed a short distance behind. He surveyed the yard in the moonlight but failed to find Jed and the girl. Fearing to cause Esther more discomfort by his presence he walked around to the other side of the porch. If I could get my hands on Jed, he thought, I wouldn't turn him loose until he explains his actions this night. His throat felt parched and he looked with longing toward the bootlegger's wagon. As if pulled by a string, he walked down the porch steps and made his way there.

CHAPTER 6

Abby

Abby McIntosh hated to see Stump go to the party without her but, truth to tell, she was too tired to care that much. A tall, thin woman with thick, raven hair in a braid down her back, she rocked her week-old son in her arms shushing his whimpering.

Stump came to her and wrapped them both in his arms. "I hate to go off and leave you with the little one when Ray is just getting over his fever, but I won't get a chance like this again soon. And you know this new batch of stump water is just crying for a home. Now, come on and give me a smile and say it's all right."

Abby managed a weak smile and laid her head on his shoulder for a moment. Nearly as tall as she, Stump stood square and solid. Her head fit into his shoulder just right, she thought, and felt mollified.

Ray woke up crying a few minutes after Stump left. Weak from childbirth and weary after a week of caring for the ailing child, Abby laid the baby in the cradle his father had fashioned for him. She sat in a low rocking chair and pushed the cradle gently with her foot. Ray climbed onto her lap and she set the chair in motion. All three of them soon slept.

Abby woke with a start. Looking around at the darkened house, she realized she had been asleep for several hours. No lamp had she lighted, but moonlight streamed through the windows. Then she heard the clip-clop of horse's hooves and knew why she had wakened. Five sharp cracks of gunfire sent chills down her spine. She clasped her sleeping son more closely. Sound of rapid hoof beats quickly faded but terror still gripped Abby and she remained motionless a few minutes longer.

Then curiously replaced terror. She laid the sleeping child on the bed and peered out the window facing the road. The scene she saw made her weep: Matt Conover knelt in the dusty road and lifted the lifeless body of his son Paul in his arms. From this distance she could not see Paul well enough to identify him, but she recognized his horse. The horse lowered his head near the two men and nickered softly.

Jerking the door open and running to them, she said, "Bring him in the house, Matt."

Matt gently placed his son back on the ground. Tears streamed down his face as he said, "No, he's gone. Bring something to cover him, please."

She hurried to bring a quilt and covered the young man. As she rose from her knees, she saw her husband racing toward them. Sobbing helplessly, she stood rooted to the spot. He came to her and held her as if she were a child.

A hubbub of voices announced the arrival of other men. Ben Conover placed his hand on his father's arm and said, "Pa, what is it?"

Matt shook his head as if to clear it while he searched for an answer. As he hesitated, Jed rounded the corner out of breath. He slid to a stop, bent over and grasped a corner of the quilt.

"Don't touch it!" Matt pulled Jed away, then put an arm around each of his sons. Voice breaking, he said, "It's Paul. We must not disturb the scene until the authorities see it." Turning to the crowd, he asked, "Has anyone gone after the sheriff?"

CHAPTER 7

Buford

Buford Conover had expected either Al or Camp Sexton to relieve him of his watch at the corral long before sundown. He watched the moon rise with a growing anger. When the two men left him early that morning after all three had spent the night filching horses from the surrounding area, they had promised that one of them would return that afternoon so he could go home.

He had eaten the last of his food at noon. Gnawing hunger increased his anger. He walked once again to the little creek at the bottom of the hill and drank. The creek was almost dry after the summer's drought and the water tasted brackish. Sand gritted in his teeth and he cursed aloud.

As the moon rode higher in the sky, he reckoned that two hours had passed since moonrise. Apprehension mingled with his anger as he paced back and forth. This venture marked his first association with the Sexton brothers. Both men had a reputation for viciousness. He had seen the cruel way they treated the stolen horses last night. Deep in his heart he was afraid of them and wished that he had never gotten mixed up with them. Paying off his gambling debts posed such a problem that he had taken the easy way out. Or so it had seemed at the time.

Old Bob had curled up to sleep earlier but he roused suddenly and sat up cocking his head to one side as if listening. The horses milled around in the corral. Buford heard an approaching horse then and lost no time in saddling his own horse. He prepared to mount as Camp Sexton rode into the clearing.

"It's about time," he said as he swung into the saddle.

Camp's body stiffened and he laid his hand on the butt of his rifle. "You'd do well to watch your language, Bub. Remember who's the boss of this outfit."

Buford's temper flared. "I thought it was Al. He's the oldest."

Camp pulled the rifle from its scabbard and jumped from his horse. "I'm only going to warn you once. You do or say anything to queer this deal and you won't be the only one who will suffer. Now git."

Buford kicked his horse in the flanks and hurdled into the brush with Old Bob scampering along beside him. Expending no effort to be quiet, he rode as fast as the heavy growth allowed. Once he reached the road, he put the horse into a trot until he approached Sid Drumm's place. Moving into the woods, he eased the animal down to a walk and followed the old track to his home.

He was surprised that no light shone in the house and saw that the bed in the yard also was unoccupied. Lighting a lamp, he went directly to the stove and looked in the warming oven for food. Seeing plenty of vegetables, he set the lamp on the table and proceeded to fill a plate. He poured a tall glass with fresh buttermilk and fell to.

Supper finished, Buford looked around for a note. Customarily his family left notes under the lamp on the dresser in the sleeping quarters of the main room, but he had not found one when he lighted the lamp. He took the lamp and hunted until he found it on a table beside the front door. Pa must have taken it outside to find a better light for his failing eyesight. He cleaned up, saddled his horse, and took the main road to the party.

When he reached the corner by the McIntosh farmhouse, he heard noise down the side road. It sounded like voices rising and falling. Deciding to investigate, he came upon a strange scene. A group of men along with the Indian woman, Abby McIntosh, milled around a quilt-covered object that looked suspiciously like a body. Cold chills quivered up his spine and a hard knot of dread grabbed his midsection. He knew who lay under the quilt even before he saw his father and two brothers in the crowd. But he had to ask.

Ben spoke quietly. "It's Paul. He's been ambushed."

Hot anger chased the cold chills away. He spoke before he thought. "I know who did this. I'll kill the sons—"

"Buford!" Matt's voice of authority cut his epithet short. "There's a lady present," his father finished mildly.

But Matt's warning had come too late. Chuck Timmons, the deputy sheriff, had left his horse a distance away and quietly entered the crowd. Walking up to Buford, he said, "If you know who did this, you tell the authorities, not the whole country. Stick around, I'll talk to you after I know what's going on."

Buford struggled with conflicting emotions. Fear for his own life dominated when he looked at the body of his brother. Love and loss swelled within him as the reality of Paul's death hit him. "I don't know why I spouted off," he told the deputy. "I don't know anything about it."

Timmons didn't buy it. "Stick around like I told you."

"Now, anybody who knows something for sure, please step forward."

Matt Conover went to his side.

"Anyone else?"

Stump McIntosh led his wife to the deputy. "She don't want you to talk to her in front of these men. We're going in the house. You can come in when you're ready."

Timmons nodded assent and turned to the curious onlookers. "Anybody that has no business here, leave." He turned to Matt. "I understand that he is your son. Then your boys can stay, too."

Matt looked at his boys. "Ben, go get your mother and the rest of the family. Take them home. Tell them what happened but don't bring them here. You'll have to watch Holt, he'll slip away from you and I don't want him to see this. He's too young."

After Ben left, Timmons again ordered the stragglers to leave. Reluctantly they obeyed. Then he turned to Matt. "You realize you'll have to repeat everything you tell me to the sheriff when he gets here tomorrow, but I want to hear it while it's still fresh in your mind. I know you've been a lawman yourself, so just tell it in your own words."

Buford had been wondering why the deputy had allowed Paul's family to stay. Anxiety settled in the pit of his stomach, cramping and roiling. He sensed that the deputy hadn't finished questioning him and felt startled when Timmons questioned his father.

Matt cleared his throat and Timmons said, "I understand you found the, uh—Paul."

"Yes. I was on my way to Wilson's. I cut across McIntosh's land—I rent an eighty from him—and was about halfway to his house when I heard the shots. Five, I counted. Then I heard horses beating it down the road. Just two, I reckon, but I could be wrong."

Matt cleared his throat again and wiped his eyes with a thumb and middle finger. "I stepped as quiet as I could until I was in sight of the house. Not a sign of life did I see; no light, no horses or wagon. Making as little sound as possible, I passed to the road. Right in front of their house, I saw him. I recognized the clothes, the same ones he had on this morning when I left. I knew I shouldn't disturb anything, but, Sheriff, he's my boy. I raised his shoulders and head up in my arms...." His voice broke and he choked on the words. He bowed his head as his body shook with sobs but no sound escaped.

Buford felt helpless. He stood rooted to the spot swallowing again and again.

Jed went to his father and put an arm around his shoulders but Matt shook him off and finished his story.

"I said my good-byes." His tight voice and rigid body evidenced the effort he put into his control. "Then I laid him back as he was. Mrs. McIntosh came out then and I asked her to being something to cover him."

"You didn't see anyone?"

"No, not until Abby—Missus McIntosh. Stump got there about the time Abby brought the quilt, but he said he heard the shots while he was at Wilson's. Then Ben ran up with all the others not far behind him."

"Matt, I hate to leave your son here the rest of the night, but I want the sheriff to see the scene. It's been disturbed enough with all the milling around. Some of your family can stay here with him. I'll go by the undertaker's when I get back to town and notify him. I'll get word to the sheriff tonight or early in the morning. I think he'll leave as soon as he gets the report and you can expect him to be here early. You and Buford plan on meeting him here."

Buford felt a sense of dread and impending doom. His queasy stomach felt as if a rock had been dropped into it and plunged to the bottom. He looked around for his horse and found it standing asleep beside the road. Paul's horse had come back earlier and walked toward his master. Jed caught him and tethered him to a tree in McIntosh's yard. Occasionally he breathed a mournful whinny that sent cold chills down Buford's back.

After Chuck Timmons bid them goodnight and went into the house to interview Abby, Matt took over. Buford thought he sounded like a cross between a father and a Texas Ranger on a case.

Matt approached Jed and faced the nineteen-year-old squarely. "Jed, I hate to ask you to stay here by yourself with Paul, but I want Buford to go with me. We need to get home. Your mother—I don't know how your mother will take this. I have to ask you to be a man now. It will be a long night and black dark when the moon goes down but I know you can handle it and I'm counting on you."

He turned to Buford. "I'll ride Paul's horse. Let's go home."

As soon as they were out of Jed's hearing, Matt confronted Buford. "You know a whole lot more about this than you let on back there. You're mixed up with those sorry Sextons and I want you to come clean with me."

Buford felt the way he did when he was six years old and got caught stealing Paul's Christmas candy. "I don't know what you're getting at, Pa. I didn't have anything to do with Paul's death."

"Oh, yes, you did. Paul told me this morning that he saw you and the Sexton boys stealing Sid Drumm's horses last night. He wanted to turn you in but he hated to do that to his own brother. He asked me what to do."

Buford started to defend himself but thought better of it. He had learned a long time ago to wait for his father to ask direct questions.

They reached home before Matt said softly as if he were talking to himself, "I told him we'd discuss it when I got home tonight."

Flora and Ida ran to meet them as soon as they heard the hoofbeats. Both of the men slid from their saddles and embraced the sobbing girls.

"I can't believe it," Flora said. "Pa, tell me it's not true." She buried her head in her father's shoulder.

"I wish I could, but I can't lie to you. How is your Ma?"

Buford felt great spasms course through his body as he held the weeping Ida. "Buck up, little sister. You have to be brave."

"Oh, Buford, for this to happen on my birthday of all times. I'll remember this terrible night every birthday as long as I live."

Buford thought, So will I, if I have another birthday.

Matt said, "Buford, you and Ida go on in the house and see what you can do for your Ma. Flora can help me. We'll take care of your horse."

That puzzled Buford. If there was one thing Pa had always taught them, it was to pull their own weight. He thought of protesting but the tone of his father's voice warned him to obey. He had turned to follow Ida into the house when Matt called him back.

"On second thought, Son, I need you to get me another shirt. Don't one of you boys have a clean one in the dugout that will fit me?"

It hit him then. Pa had picked up Paul and held him in his arms. He didn't know how many of the five shots had hit their mark, but Paul must have been bleeding. Without hesitation he unbuttoned his own shirt and pulled it off. "Here, Pa. I put this on clean just tonight. I'll get the one I wore today. Ma doesn't know which one either of us was wearing. You go to Ma and I'll draw the water for Flora to soak your shirt. You don't worry about a thing. We'll take care of it."

Matt buttoned the clean shirt and tucked it in his waistband. Then he hugged Buford hard and said to Flora, "Sister, I don't like to give this grievous task to you but I don't know what else to do."

Flora said, "I can manage it, Pa. I'd rather have something to do."

To Buford she said, "Go take care of the horses. I'll get a bucket and draw the water and soak the shirt. I'll set it in the barn overnight and finish up in the morning."

Buford gladly left the task up to her. He thought how Flora had grown up just since they had left Texas. All of the family depended on her now instead of their frail Ma. He wished he had someone at a time like this to share his own load.

What a *fix* he had blundered into. His primary instinct told him to get as far away from here as possible and right now. Camp had made a threatening gesture toward him. If it had been Al, Buford's gut told him it might have been death. Certain he was that the two had ambushed and murdered Paul. What was to keep them from doing the same to him? Pulling him is the other direction rose the prospect of his family's duties in the next few days. How could he go before they buried his brother? He needed his part of the money from selling the horses, but he feared the Sexton brothers too much even to see them let alone ask for money.

He shut the horses in their stalls after feeding and watering them. Flora finished at the same time. Buford extinguished the lantern and they trudged together toward the family conference he dreaded.

His parents, Ben and Ida sat around the dining table. Matt's big right hand engulfed Lillie's petite one and Ben patted her other arm as she dabbed at her eyes with a wadded-up handkerchief. Ida had been resting her head on her crossed arms on the table but she raised up when she heard the door open. Tears streamed down her face and she tried to wipe them on her sleeve.

Flora reached in her pocket and handed Ida a handkerchief. She then went to her room and soon returned with a handful of printed handkerchiefs. Buford knew that it was her collection given by friends at handkerchief parties and that she had never used any of them before.

Pity gripped his heart as he looked at the grief of his family. Pangs of conscience overwhelmed him as he pondered his part in this tragedy. He said the first thing that came to mind. "Where are the little ones?"

Ben answered, "Asleep. We put Betsy to bed in Ma and Pa's room and Holt piled up in the bed out there in the yard."

Matt said, "The rest of us might as well get some sleep, too. We can't make any plans till morning."

Ben rose and stretched. "I don't think I can sleep a wink. I'll go relieve Jed. We may both stay all night. Don't worry if he'd rather stay, too." He closed the door softly behind him when he left.

Matt pulled Lillie to her feet and said to the girls, "Y'all go on to bed now. Buford and I have to go early to wait for the sheriff. We don't want him to have to send for us when he gets here. Ida, Holt can help you with the milking while Flora fixes breakfast. Just do what chores have to be done and feed and water the animals. We'll pick no cotton tomorrow."

He waited until the sisters closed the door to their room before he led his wife to their own door. Then, fixing Buford in his tracks with the authority in his voice, he said, "Stick around a minute, Son. I want to talk to you."

Buford sweated out the minute that seemed to stretch into hours. He paced the floor and marshaled his excuses. It was not the first time that Pa had grilled him and he dreaded it. Pa's years as a Texas Ranger had taught him all the hard questions.

When Matt appeared again, he picked up a lantern and said, "Let's go to the barn. I don't want anybody to hear us."

In the barn, he lighted the lantern and hung it on its hook. Buford noticed that the light shone full on his own face after Matt moved into shadow. He felt uncomfortable but didn't see what he could do about it.

Matt said, "To be fair to you, I'll first tell you what I know. Paul told me this morning that he followed you and the Sexton boys last night and saw you drive off several of Sid Drumm's horses. He had tied his horse a distance away so he was afoot and since you were on horseback, he couldn't keep up with you and didn't know where you went with them. He did know for sure that you hadn't come home all night.

"He was in a quandary what to do. If it had been only the Sextons, he would have turned them in. He couldn't bring himself to do that to his own brother. At least he was wrestling with his conscience about it. He asked me what to do."

Matt paused but Buford sensed that he had more to say. He waited for several minutes before his father continued.

"I stalled. I told him we'd talk when I got home tonight." His voice broke and Buford knew in his heart the words Matt couldn't say; *we'll never talk again.*

Buford thought, the sight of my brother lying in the dust made me angry, the sound of my sister's sobbing made me pity her, but I cannot bear to see my strong father broken by grief. He buried his face in his hands and wept.

The spasm of weeping finished, he asked, "What do you want to know?"

"You said you knew who killed Paul. Tell me how."

"I'm guilty of everything Paul told you. We took the horses about five miles back in the thick woods to a little clearing we had fenced off. I was to keep watch today with one of the boys to relieve me late afternoon. About time for him to arrive, what should come rushing out of the woods but Uncle Prent's squirrel dog? Right behind him, slipping through the undergrowth as quiet as a mouse, was Paul. When he saw I was by myself, he walked up to me and accused me of the theft. I was scared to death that he was going to get caught. I kept warning him and warning him. He finally left but Old Bob stayed with me.

"Well, Camp finally relieved me way after dark. I came home and ate something, found the note, and started to the party. As soon as I saw the quilt-covered body, I knew it was Paul and also knew why Camp Sexton was so late. There was no question in my mind, then or now."

Matt nodded and said, "That settles it then. We'll tell the sheriff in the morning. You'll have to pay for your part in the matter, but it's all we can do. I got you out of Texas and the trouble you were in, but this is different. Your brother lies dead at the hand of your compatriots. It's time for you to stand up like a man, take your medicine, and change your ways."

Buford hung his head. His father patted his arm and said, "Let's go try to get some sleep now. Are you going to bunk with Holt?"

"No, Pa, I think I'll go to the dugout. I need to be alone awhile."

CHAPTER 8

Matt

A half-hour before daybreak the next morning Matt shook Holt awake. The boy was a sleepyhead like his brother Jed and his father sat on the bed until he knew Holt wouldn't go back to sleep. "You'll have to help your sister milk this morning. Flora got up and fixed breakfast extra early so I could eat before I had to leave. Go on in and get your breakfast before you go to milk. I'm going to wake Buford up now so we can be on our way."

Holt interrupted him. "Buford's not here, Pa. He left during the night. I was awake but I didn't let on. He loaded his saddlebags and bedroll and led his horse away. I think he's gone for good."

Matt felt a flood of anger. I should have watched Buford, he thought, but he seemed so contrite last night that I let down my guard. I never could abide a coward and now I have to admit that I raised one.

He watched the door open and close as Holt went in for breakfast. Alone for the first time since he saw Abby McIntosh appear at his side last night, he sank down on the bed and buried his face in his hands. He felt the weight of the world on his shoulders. His anger had subsided and in its place he felt an unbearable grief. He thought of his family one by one and wondered how the events of the past night would affect each one.

Lillie, my sweet frail Lillie, this will tear you to pieces. Will you lose your mind over it the way you did when Terence died? How can I sustain you when I can't bear my own burden?

Buford, my wayward son, what fear you must feel to run off and not even go to the funeral of your murdered brother. I've protected you as long as I aim to. This day I'll tell the sheriff all you told me. They'll come after you, my son. This time you'll have to stand trial for the thieving you've committed. I can't believe I didn't hear you when you left last night. It must have been one of the times I dozed for a few minutes.

Always before when he called the roll of his family from oldest to youngest, Paul commanded third place. It's no different this time, Matt thought. This day will see your burying, my ambitious son. You always wanted to be a lawman but you just didn't have the feel for it. You couldn't follow clues or gather evidence. You tried so hard but you never would have made it.

Matt sighed as he pushed himself to his feet. Weariness limned his body like an aura. His shoulders sagged and his neck felt too limp to hold his head up. With a great effort of will he turned his steps toward the barn. He must saddle a horse and face this hard, hard day. He had already bid his family goodbye when he finished breakfast. He had told them to prepare for a funeral and that he would be back as soon as the sheriff released Paul's body.

The promise of day lightened the eastern sky as Matt turned west onto the new county road. He had not gone far when he encountered Plez and Polly Wilson carrying cotton sacks. He stopped and greeted them.

Plez said, "We are so sorry for your loss, Mr. Conover. Paul was my best friend in this world, I reckon."

Polly bowed her head gazing at her feet, and said nothing. She had visited his home often and Matt was surprised that she didn't speak to him. It's that Indian reserve coming out in her, he thought. Then he saw a tear splash in the dust and knew Paul's death had struck a blow. I wonder if they were sparking, he thought. I haven't had any inkling of it.

He said, "You know I'm much obliged but you didn't have to leave your own work."

Plez said, "We didn't plant a crop of cotton this year, Mr. Conover. We can help you out through this hardship."

"Well, I'm mighty obliged. Y'all plan on going to the house for dinner. I'm sure Flora will be cooking at noon."

"No, Sir. We brought our own meal."

Matt noticed for the first time that Polly carried a bucket. He hardly knew what to say to such kindness and thoughtfulness. "I'll say goodbye then. I need to get on about my business. Thank you again."

They parted and Matt proceeded on his way but soon stopped again when he met a wagon loaded with all seven of the McMasters family. He raised a forefinger to his hat and said to Everett McMasters, "Howdy, you're out early this morning."

McMasters returned his greeting. "We're headed for your place. Are some of your folks there who can tell us where to pick today?"

Matt felt tears sting his eyes. He had to swallow before he could answer. Many a time he himself had left his own work to help a neighbor in trouble, but had not experienced being on the receiving end since Lillie's breakdown when Terence died. He repeated his earlier expression of gratitude. "Much obliged; I'm indebted to you. I left Jed to sit up with Paul last night and Ben joined him. When I get there, I'll send Jed home. He can show you where to pick. Now y'all be sure to take dinner with the family. Flora will have a meal ready by noon."

"Thank you, but we brought our own victuals." McMasters squinted at the sky. "It's about sunup. We'd best get in the field."

Matt thanked them again and rode on his way.

When he arrived at the scene of the shooting, he found Stump McIntosh conversing with his two sons. Tying his horse to a tree on the roadside, he joined the group. All three men extended a hand in greeting. He was taken aback at such an uncharacteristic gesture from his sons. His family expressed their feelings freely when alone and he supposed their reticence due to the presence of the outsider.

He shook hands with McIntosh first, then with each of his boys in turn. He could barely keep from embracing them. Jed's grip hurt Matt's hand and Matt thought it expressed more restrained feeling than a hug would have. My impulsive son has become a man overnight, he thought.

Ben's firm handshake echoed Matt's own. We are so much alike, Matt thought. This is my dependable son. I probably depend on him too much. He has been a man a long time.

"You boys must be hungry. Go on home and eat breakfast. Flora's keeping it hot for you."

Ben said, "Missus McIntosh fed us awhile ago. Where is Buford? I thought he'd come with you."

Matt hesitated. He hated to mention Buford's disappearance in front of their landlord.

Apparently sensing the reason for Matt's hesitation, Stump McIntosh said, "I'll be seeing to my stock. I need to have it all done when the sheriff gets here. Abby is worried to death about what he'll ask her. I want to be with her."

After he left, Matt spoke bluntly. "Buford skipped the country last night. I asked him if he wanted to sleep in the yard with Holt but he went to the dugout. He said he wanted to be alone for a while. I didn't hear any more out of him, but Holt saw him load his bedroll and saddlebags and slip out.

"You boys probably don't know that Paul was on the trail of the Sexton boys for stealing horses. Buford was right in the middle of the whole sorry mess. Paul confronted Buford and Buford is sure that one of the Sexton brothers came up on them and heard their conversation. That's why Buford started to spout off last night. Luckily I saw the deputy ease into the crowd in time to cut Buford off before he finished."

Jed cut in, "What do you intend to tell the sheriff?"

"Well, I've mulled it over in my mind and I intend to tell him everything I know. It's all hearsay but it should give them enough information to arrest Al and Camp Sexton. They'll go after Buford, too, and bring him back when they catch him. I hate to see this day for more than one reason. All I can hope for is that they don't hang Buford."

Matt looked from one to the other of his sons. "How did you boys do last night? Anybody come by?"

Jed said, "Nope. Some small animals snooped around after the moon went down but I scared them off. It was pretty spooky when it got so dark but pretty soon Ben showed up and we spent the night talking."

Matt said, "I'm sorry I had to put such a burden on you but I'm afraid this is just the start of it. Jed, I met the young Wilsons and the whole McMasters family going to work in our fields today. You know where we're ready to pick so you go home and show them. They all brought their own grub, but if any other neighbors come, they might need to eat with our family. See that Flora knows and fixes a good dinner."

Matt laid a hand on Ben's arm. "Ben, I'd like you to stay with me. We'll have to make arrangements about burying Paul when the sheriff releases him."

Ben had hardly said a word but after Jed left, he said, "Pa, I know you've got enough on your mind but I have a confession to make. I lost Uncle Prent's dog. I let him come with me intending to take him home when I go back. He disappeared yesterday just before we got here and I haven't seen hide nor hair of him since. We should keep an eye out while we make our rounds today."

"He was at the place last night when Buford and I went home. He came bounding out of the barn to meet us. But, come to think of it, he wasn't around this morning. I'll bet he went with Buford."

At that moment they heard muffled hoofbeats and the sheriff soon appeared along with the deputy and the undertaker. They alighted from their horses and led them to the horse trough to drink. When they had tied them at the roadside, they turned toward the draped body lying in the road.

Matt went forward to meet them but Ben hung back. Chuck Timmons introduced the two men. "Sheriff Pickens, this is Matt Conover. I've told you about him; he used to be a Texas Ranger."

They shook hands and the sheriff said, "I'm terribly sorry for your loss and I want to thank you for your co-operation. First I would like to see the body. Will that work too much of a hardship on you?"

"No, I can take it but I don't know about my son, Ben, here. He's been sitting up with his brother's body and hasn't had any sleep after his trip up from Texas. He just got in yesterday afternoon."

Ben stepped forward and the sheriff extended his hand to him. "You don't have to look if you'd rather not. I take it that you are not a witness in any way."

"No, I'm not a witness but I think I will look. I'll have to get used to his death some time and I might as well start now."

Matt said, "He's pretty shot up in the upper body, but I didn't see any damage to his head. I'll tell you up front that I picked him up in my arms but I put him back as carefully as I could."

Sheriff Pickens picked up the quilt by a corner and lifted it. He peered under it then threw it back uncovering Paul's entire body. He and Deputy Timmons then lifted him and laid him on the quilt face down. He motioned to the undertaker to make his examination and determine the feasibility of embalming.

Mr. Bryce shook his head and spoke to Matt and Ben. "You know we have had a law in this territory for over ten years that requires embalming instead of the old way. But I think in this case that the best thing is to schedule the burial soon after the sheriff is through here. I can lay him out for you and provide a coffin, if it's agreeable to you. I have instructed my helper to bring a hearse. He should be arriving at any time. Perhaps you would like to get the clothing for his burial."

Matt said, "Yes, that's what would be best. His mother is frail, you know, and I want to save her as much grief as I can."

To Ben, he said, "Go home and get Paul's suit and a shirt and the black string tie he loved to wear. Bring it back so they can take it back to town with them. You can probably make faster time if you cut through McIntosh's woods."

Mr. Bryce said, "That's settled then. I suggest you plan to have the funeral tomorrow morning. Do you have a preacher?"

"Yes, Mr. Goodgion is the preacher where my daughter goes. We'll have him. Will you be bringing Paul home today?"

"I'll be there as soon as I can. I take it you will bury him from home. What cemetery do you want me to use?"

"Which one is the closest?"

"Pendleton. I can arrange for the grave to be opened, too. Is this all satisfactory?"

"Yes."

Mr. Bryce extended his hand again. "I extend my sympathies to you and your family. This is a terrible thing. I'll do all I can to lighten your burden."

By the time Ben returned with the clothing, Sheriff Pickens and Deputy Timmons had finished interviewing Matt and had gone into the house to talk with Abby McIntosh. The hearse had arrived in Ben's absence and Paul's body had been loaded. Matt turned from his conversation with Mr. Bryce and said to Ben, "I'll take the horse and ride in with Mr. Bryce to make the final arrangements. I'll be back before long, but you go on home and see to your Ma. I hope she'll be up to deciding on arranging the house for the funeral. If not, you and the girls will have to buck up and see to it yourselves.

You're awfully young for such responsibility but I have confidence in you."

Mr. Bryce joined the driver in the horse-drawn hearse and they departed. Matt embraced his son and said, "I'm going on now. I can travel faster than the hearse, but I think I'll go by the cemetery on the way. Be a man and take care of the family until I get home. You're the oldest now with Buford gone." He put his hand on Ben's shoulder and squeezed. "Son, I'm so glad you're home."

CHAPTER 9

Ben

When Ben had gone after Paul's clothes, he cut across McIntosh's pasture and into the woods rather than travel the road. Certain he was out of sight of any other human, he leaned against a tree and let all his pent-up emotions have full sway. From the time he realized Old Bob had disappeared yesterday afternoon, he had been bombarded with one intense feeling after another. He thought if he didn't take time to absorb them that he would explode.

    He had counted on the need to take the dog home for an excuse to return to Texas. Once there, he had no intention of returning to Indian Territory. He hated everything about leaving the only home he had ever known and the state he loved. He didn't want to leave his many childhood friends as well as his slew of cousins. They had all grown up together and had turned their childhood diversions into more adult pastimes. He reveled in remembering the Fourth District horse race he had recently won and the roping contest he had lost in such close competition that he knew he could win next year. If he didn't get back home by the start of baseball season, what would his county team do for a shortstop? And he already missed his drinking and poker buddies. He had his eye on several girls, too.

However, all his longing and high hopes of returning home had disappeared in a flash last night when he first saw Esther McMasters. Never had his heart done such a flip-flop. Even now when he pictured her, a thrill traveled from the top of his head to the soles of his feet. Before Jed strode into the picture, his imagination had already envisioned himself and Esther as a pair. Being dashed from the heights of anticipation to the depths of hopelessness in one hour had driven him to a need to drown his feelings. He was beginning to count out money for a jar of moonshine when the sound of gunshots intervened and he had run behind Stump McIntosh to the horrible scene of his brother's ambush.

Memory of the night just passed caused him to slide down the tree trunk into a sitting position. He rested his elbows on his knees and buried his face in his hands as he allowed all the sensations he had felt to flow over him. Horror gripped him again when he thought of Paul's sudden end in such a dastardly fashion. Regret almost too great to bear flooded him and he thought, I didn't even get to see him alive, I'll never get to say another word to him. Grief broke through in a flood and he cried until he felt exhausted.

Then he thought of his father and saw again the droop of his shoulders and heard the tears in his voice. This has made an old man of Pa even though he is still in charge. Man, don't I *know* he's still in charge. He felt both pity and admiration for Matt.

And that brought him to the rest of the family. No one knows what will happen to Ma over this, he thought, and felt like he wanted to kill Buford with his own hands. He's the cause of all this grief and has taken the coward's way out. Flora will be all right; she has grown up while I was gone. But I don't know about Ida. She is flighty at best and thinks everyone and every circumstance is against her. I guess Jed's got Esther to soften the blow for him. Holt is at an age that he'll need guidance; I'll have to help him. Only Betsy is too little to be affected by this unless Ma starts having her spells again. That'll scare the britches off her.

He began to feel calmer and pushed himself slowly to his feet. Before he took a step, he observed Jed walk purposefully to a tree in the woods and stick his hand into a hole in the trunk. The tree was within twenty feet of Ben and he was surprised that Jed had not seen him. "Whatcha hunting, Little Brother?" he said.

Jed jumped as though he had been shot and turned around. When he saw Ben, he moved closer and said, "I'll tell you what's going on if you won't tell anybody. This is one of the two hiding places Esther and I have for passing notes." He paused as if considering whether to reveal more. "You know, Esther grew up in this nation and didn't have a chance to go to school. So I've been teaching her to read and write. We hide notes. This is the tree we hide notes in over here. And we have another tree where we hide notes at her place. I was just checking to see if she had hid one for me today. You'll have to get to know her, Ben. I know you'll love her."

Ben felt as if Jed had knocked the wind out of him. His confidences about Esther were more than Ben wanted to hear. I don't think I can get over it, he thought, so I'll have to learn to hide it. He changed the subject. "Pa sent me after burying clothes for Paul. I'll get his suit and string tie, but we may have to find a clean shirt no matter which one of us it belongs to. Go with me to pick one out. You and I are the only ones left of us four older boys now." Misery choked him and he swallowed before he could go on. "Have you noticed how this has aged Pa?"

Jed nodded and stood silent. He removed his hat and clutched the brim with both hands, turning it around and around.

Ben thought, Jed is really taking it hard. I've never seen him when he was at a loss for words.

The two men began walking toward their home. When they reached the edge of the woods, Ben put his hand on Jed's arm. "How's Ma taking it?"

"I've been in the cotton patch all morning and haven't seen her. Pa told me to see that Flora fixed dinner for all the neighbors who came without victuals, but she came out to the field so I didn't have to go to the house. I haven't seen Ma since it happened and I sure do dread it. Can't we just go to the dugout and pick up a shirt? I need to get back to work."

Ben reckoned he dreaded seeing his mother as much as Jed did. That's how different we are, he thought. I wade right in and face unpleasantness and get it over with while Jed puts it off as long as he can. I don't blame him in this situation, though. I wish I didn't have to go in the house to get Paul's suit.

He said, "Let's go then. We'll get a shirt and you get back to work. I'll go in and get the rest of the clothes we need." He touched Jed's shoulder and patted it. "Little Brother, these next few hours will be the worst we've ever faced. It'll be hard on the whole family. I reckon it's up to you and me to be strong and soften the blow for Ma and Pa as much as we can. We'll lean on each other."

Jed wiped his eyes with his sleeve, then ran his left hand over his hair as he put his hat on with his right hand in one fluid motion. The familiar gesture seemed to give him the strength he needed because he squared his shoulders and strode forward.

That's more like you, Ben thought, and hurried to catch up with his brother.

CHAPTER 10

Jed

Jed and Ben were surprised to find Paul's clothing neatly placed on the bed he had shared with Jed. The sight of his suit, string tie, socks, and a freshly laundered shirt hit Jed like a slam to the solar plexus. It convinced him of the reality of his brother's death more than last night's vigil. During the night he had managed to push the event to the back of his mind and concentrate on other things. He certainly had other things to ponder.

Ben's voice interrupted his thoughts. "One of the girls had to wash this shirt and iron it dry to have it ready so early. I bet it was Flora. But how did she know what to do? Is Ma up to telling her?"

Jed decided the remark needed no reply. Instead he said, "Looks like it's all under control. I'm going back to work."

I guess it's against my nature to linger on disturbing problems, Jed thought. Like last night I just put Paul out of my mind even though he lay there right in front of me. I looked at the quilt covering him and told myself Pa must have been mistaken. After all, I hadn't seen him with my own eyes. I had enough problems of my own to think on.

Jed's feet shuffled along at the edge of the harvested field nearest the farmyard. He slouched with hands in pockets and head bowed.

Slowly making his way back to the workers, he let his thoughts return to the biggest problem he had ever faced.

Vinnie's appearance at the dance had upset him from the start. Many people thought she was brazen to come uninvited because of her bad reputation but he knew her well enough to see through her performance. Deep down she was backward and it took all the grit she could muster to show up at a place where she knew she was not wanted.

He had been avoiding her for the past month. For a long time his conscience had nagged him to rid himself of her and quit leading a double life. Every time he saw Esther he grew more and more in love with her and knew he wanted to spend the rest of his life with her. He did not feel he could ask her to marry him until he broke all ties with Vinnie and made sure that he would not go back. It's all lust with Vinnie, he thought. But the unspoken words brought back scenes with her and he knew she still had power over him.

Last night when she insisted on seeing him in front of all his family and friends, he knew his secret would soon out. But it was her secret that rocked him back on his heels. He couldn't believe his ears when she whispered to him there on the dance floor. Oblivious of the impression he created, he pushed her outside away from any ears that could pick up a hint of what she said.

Once on the porch, he had looked around for a solitary location. A few couples were scattered in the yard and he could not be sure others would not follow. He shushed her when she started to talk, saying, "We'll walk down the road where we can talk in private."

Vinnie kept quiet until they were out of earshot but then her words tumbled over each other. "I haven't said this out loud to another person. I thought I should tell you first. I'm with child."

The biblical expression stunned Jed. He didn't expect her to know any scripture. Raised in a home where they studied the Bible on a more or less regular basis, he found himself using Bible terms occasionally. Every time he did so after his dalliance with Vinnie, his conscience smote him. Dalliance describes my actions exactly, he thought. Complications like pregnancy never entered my mind.

"Are you sure it's mine?"

She stopped in the middle of the road and howled. If he could, he would have bitten his tongue and recalled the words. Her wail got on his nerves. How could he stop it? He took her in his arms and smoothed her hair.

"I didn't mean it. I know better. I didn't mean it."

She didn't stop crying. He had seen his mother and sisters cry, but they wept silently, stifling sobs in a handkerchief. Vinnie cried aloud. It got louder and louder until she was almost screaming.

He tucked her head into the hollow of his shoulder smothering some of the noise and patted her until she quieted. Then he said, "I guess I'm ready to listen now. Tell me, are you sure?"

"Yeah, I'm sure. Some girls might not be but you could always set your clock by my—you know."

Jed never could get over how hard she found it to express herself in words when she certainly didn't have any problem in other ways. He waited for her to go on but she didn't. He took her hand and pulled her along until she fell into step with him. He could smell the clean scent of lye soap in her clothes and hair. He stumbled a bit as longing for her rushed over him. She fell against him and he caught her in his arms. But he remembered his firm resolve to put her out of his life and pushed her away.

"No, Vinnie, we mustn't. We need to keep our heads about us and figure out what to do."

"Do?" She whined the word. "Do? We'll get married, of course."

"Now, wait a minute. We don't know for sure that you are pregnant."

Her high-pitched wail stopped him again. He felt like putting his hand over her mouth and hoped he had pulled her far enough from the party that no one could hear her. He didn't want to silence her in the way he had just tried. That got him into too much trouble. He was afraid he'd lose his head once more. Putting his hands on her shoulders, he shook her as if she were Betsy's age.

"I didn't mean you aren't sure. But I haven't had time to absorb any of this news. I think we have to wait awhile."

She snubbed and wiped her nose on her sleeve. "You don't know what I've been through today. Ma questioned me to a fare-thee-well. I thought she was going to whip me, as big a girl as I am. She threatened to tell Pa. And you know what that means. I talked her into waiting till I talked to you.

"So, then, I started out looking for you. I ran into Plez and Paul and asked them what you were doing today. They told me you had gone to take off a load of cotton and would be gone all day. So, just to make conversation, I asked them what they were doing. They looked kind of embarrassed and said they were hunting. I found out later this afternoon about the party so I knew my family wasn't invited."

Jed's body stiffened as he realized the enormity of his dilemma. If he had to marry her, it meant bringing that whole sorry bunch into his family. Two of her older sisters had delivered "seven-month" babies. Their husbands were good-for-nothing lazy louts. Vinnie's father was known as an excellent farmer who depended on his girls for field help. She had no brothers. Jed already felt pulled in two directions. He had to get out of marrying her if he could find a way.

Vinnie evidently had waited for him to say something. When he didn't, she went on, "I knew you would show up at the party sooner or later, so when I got my chores done, I walked over there and hid back in the woods until I saw you come in. I watched all the fun and dancing and wished I could be a part of it. But I noticed something else, too. More than one couple slipped into the barn or climbed up in the back of a wagon. You high hoity-toity folks don't need to think you're so far above me.

"Then you strutted in the way you always do and took over the party. If you could see yourself and the way people fawn over you—I'd like to tell them you lead a double life. You sit in the amen corner on Sunday and meet me in the woods on Monday."

Jed could stand it no longer. "I've been trying to put all that behind me. You know we haven't been together for weeks. I've straightened out my life and I intend to keep on doing what is right. That's why I can't believe you haven't made some mistake."

She cut him off, "Some mistake, is it? We both made this mistake and in a few months this mistake will have a name. And my baby's last name is not about to be Wade. It's going to be Conover."

Jed's smoldering anger burst into flame. "What if I refuse to marry you? I don't have to, you know. For one thing, I'm nineteen. I'd either have to lie about my age or get my Pa to sign for me. I could deny ever having anything to do with you. Nobody ever saw us together. It'd be your word against mine. Who do you think everybody would believe?"

She slapped him. "It doesn't matter what everybody believes. It only matters what my Pa believes. And, let me tell you, I've seen him before in this kind of situation. You won't stand a chance."

They heard the shots then.

"I'm going to see what that's all about. You go on home," Jed said.

"No, not until you tell me you'll marry me."

"I can't tell you that tonight. Give me time to digest this news. Not that I believe you. You could be trying to trap me."

"We'll see about that. I can't keep Ma quiet forever and then the fat will be in the fire. You'd better come to some conclusion pretty soon. I'll let it go for now but our baby won't let you off the hook for very long."

Jed could still see in his mind's eye the determined set of her shoulders as she stalked off. The full moon was riding high as he turned to hurry back to the party. Most of the men had left for the scene of the shooting by then and he ran to join them.

He roused from his reverie to discover he had reached the far edge of the cotton patch. As he looked out over the field, he saw neighbors scattered in nearly every one of the quarter-mile-long rows. At the rate they picked, both wagons would be filled by midafternoon. He crisscrossed the field greeting each picker, thanking them again for helping his family in their time of need, and remarking that they should be finished soon after dinner. He asked each one again to eat the noon meal with his family but one by one they declined. He saw Flora beside Plez picking three rows between them and stopped to tell her there would be no extras for their noon meal.

"Yes, I've already asked them. They all want to know when the funeral will be. Do you know yet?"

"No, we'll know when Pa gets back. I don't see how it can be today and we can't wait too long. I'm guessing tomorrow morning but I don't know for sure."

Flora said, "Have you seen Esther yet? She's as mad as a wet hen. You'd better go see if you can make amends while you still can."

He had deliberately spoken with everyone else before Esther. He wanted to spend the rest of the morning working beside her. She had separated from the bulk of the workers having chosen to pick the rows nearest the woods. He stepped over the rustling stalks row after row until he reached her.

She ignored his presence. He stood in front of her and said, "I'll carry your sack for you. You pick the row on that side and I'll pick on this side."

She didn't pull the strap of the sack off her shoulder but kept doggedly snatching the white cotton out of the prickly bolls. She worked with both hands harvesting one or two stalks in a row before changing her position in order to reach the row on the other side of her. Her long skirt hampered her movements and she jerked it from underneath her knees.

Jed grasped the strap across her back and pulled her to her feet. She refused to face him so he took her by the shoulders and turned her. Her flushed face and tight lips showed him her fury.

"Don't be like that, Essie. I can explain."

"I doubt it. I haven't seen you since Sunday and the first thing you do is dance with that—that thing." She spat out the word as if she had taken a bite of spoiled food. "Then you leave with her and don't come back. How are you going to explain that?"

"The truth is, I felt sorry for her. You should have seen the look on the face of all the girls when she walked into that room. Yes, on your face, too. I don't know why she picked me to dance with her and I started to tell her no, but you had already shrunk away from me so fast that you'd have thought I was snake bit. And the reason I left with her was to get her away so the party could go on and everybody could start having fun again. All I did was walk her home. And I was hurrying back when I heard the shots." He choked and fell silent.

She had listened with her face stubbornly facing the ground, her shoulders drooping. The weight of the cotton sack pulled against them so that she clasped the strap in both hands to relieve the pressure. At his last words, she lifted her head and looked him full in the face. She began crying and reached out with both hands to clasp his.

Never in his life had he wanted so badly to take her in his arms. He wished they could run into the woods together so they would be out of sight of all the others. But either action would ruin her reputation. He didn't care what people thought of him but he felt he must protect Esther. He didn't know whether she had believed his story or not. He hadn't meant to play on his grief to win her over, but now that it had, he accepted it.

He squeezed her hands and said, "I think I see Pa coming home. I'd better go see what he has to tell us." His voice softened as he said, "I'd kiss you if I could. I wrote you a note. Go get it when you have a chance. I love you."

She didn't answer him in words but the tender look in her eyes sufficed him. One of the qualities he loved in her was her quiet demeanor. Not that she was solemn. Her laughter could be the gayest in any group. But when she felt any deep emotion she seemed to hug it to her heart rather put it into words. What a contrast there was between her and Vinnie. His heart twisted at the thought of Vinnie and the predicament she had presented to him last night. Was it only less than twelve hours? It seemed that a lifetime had passed since she appeared at the dance; so much had happened. When he allowed himself to think about it, he knew that his life had changed in those few short hours. But he shoved the thought aside even while he made his way to ask his father about arrangements for his brother's funeral.

CHAPTER 11

Matt

Matt set his horse's gait at a walk after he turned south from the main road to travel the half-mile to Pendleton cemetery. He had never visited the site but from long Ranger training he had mentally mapped the entire area. He knew, for instance, that the sexton of the cemetery lived less than a quarter-mile east of the gate.

In fact the man had built his new home more than forty years earlier after the original structure had burned to the ground taking the lives of his wife and two small children. The bodies were never found. Mr. Pendleton had built a fence on the foundation of the two-room cottage and had erected a monument honoring his wife and children in the center. He planted a flower garden inside the fence and had maintained it all those years. He had dedicated the clearing surrounding the central area for a community cemetery. When Matt saw it, he thought it the most beautiful resting-place he had ever seen.

He had expected to ride the extra distance to the Pendleton farmstead but instead found Pendleton in his flower garden pulling spent stalks of summer annuals. Stopping near the fence, he swung his leg over the horse's back and slid to the ground.

Pendleton had heard his approach and rose stiffly from his knees. He came through the gate pulling his glove from his right hand and extended it, saying, "Jeremiah Pendleton."

Matt shook the hand and introduced himself.

Pendleton said, "I'm glad to make your acquaintance and sorry it had to be under such sad circumstances. I heard about your boy."

Matt said, "Mr. Pendleton, I came to see if I can buy a burial site. We will need one this afternoon or in the morning."

Pendleton shook his head. "Call me Jeremiah. No, these lots are not for sale. This is a community cemetery and anyone can be buried here. The only cost is for grave digging. You can furnish your own labor and there is no cost at all. I direct the excavating but I'm unable to do the hard work anymore. I don't charge anything myself, but if you have to get professionals, it will be two and a half."

Matt appreciated the way Pendleton attended to business. He didn't think he could have endured maudlin sympathy at that time. He said, "Well, Jeremiah, if you'll show me what plots you have, I'd appreciate it. And I believe I'll want to hire professionals if you can tell me where to find someone."

"Ask the undertaker. There's always loafers on the streets, but he'll know which ones will do you a good job."

Pendleton showed him an area with no graves. "You'll want to have a place big enough for you and your missus, too," he said.

Matt agreed to accept the space Pendleton pointed out and mounted his horse. He felt he couldn't get out of there fast enough. So many years he had borne the burden of his wife's frailty but he always pushed the thought of losing her to the back of his mind. The possibility lay like an ugly monster in his subconscious. It was a dark place he refused to enter. On this bright September morning he had doggedly hid his grief under a cover of busy work. Now one unintentional remark had jerked that cover not only from the present loss but also from the hidden monster.

No one knew the struggle he had experienced in the years after they lost Terence. Even after Lillie had recovered enough to function, she had undergone spells when the darkness returned and it was all he could do to keep her from falling off the edge again. Those times he had relied on Ben to stay with her during the daytime. The boy had a calming influence on her. Most times after a day with Ben she had regained her composure or whatever you wanted to call it. It had been years since one of her spells had occurred but Matt could never be sure when she might have another one. He remembered his mother saying, "I just listen for something to happen" and thought it described his feeling exactly.

He hoped Ben had followed his orders and looked after his mother. Matt had reminded him after Ben brought the clothing for Paul to be buried in. The undertaker had been ready to leave and they had caught him just in time. Matt thought, well, back to business. I still have to arrange all the details. He clucked his horse into a road trot.

On the way into Chagris, Matt stopped at Preacher Goodgion's house. Mrs. Goodgion rounded the corner from the back yard and hurried to meet him. Drying her hands on her apron, she tucked stray white hairs into the knot on the back of her head, only to have them fall out immediately. The heat and humidity of late September had taken over the day and her plump florid face reflected it. Talking as she came, she said, "I was just around back doing up Mr. Goodgion's white linen shirt. He likes the way I starch it and I want it fresh for the funeral."

Extending her right hand in greeting, she waited for him to alight from his saddle to shake it. "I'm so sorry to hear about your loss, Mr. Conover," she said. "I've sent one of my boys after Mr. Goodgion. He's holding a protracted meeting at Reck, you know. They'll just have to do without him tonight. He knows how to handle that. He'll tell them to have scripture reading, singing, and prayer and come back tomorrow night when he will resume the meeting." She paused for breath. "How I do run on. Tie your horse and come sit on the porch while I fix you a cool drink."

"I'd like that, Mrs. Goodgion. Can I draw the water for you?"

"Why, yes, if you don't mind. I just took fresh bread from the oven. Would you eat a piece with some butter?"

Matt, surprised by his sudden hunger, nodded gratefully.

"Good," Mrs. Goodgion said, "I'll hand you the bucket out the back door, then. I'd invite you in but I'm here by myself. And it's cooler outside, anyway."

She disappeared through the front door. Matt smiled and thought how she does run on. He pondered whether that was her nature or something she had developed from years of being a preacher's wife. He realized it was the first thought he'd had that day that didn't bear on the sad arrangements for Paul's funeral. He felt the heavy load on his shoulders and thought, So many years I have carried the bulk of the weight of every major crisis, every crucial decision, and the constant care of my large family. I don't know how much longer I can go on.

After drawing the water, he carried the bucket and dipper to the front porch setting it on a wicker table between two cane-bottom rockers. Mrs. Goodgion appeared carrying a tray with a loaf of bread, bowl of butter, and compote of cooked fruit. Steam rose from the bread as she tried slicing it with a butcher knife. Halfway through the loaf, she stopped and tore the heel end from the rest of the loaf.

"It's too hot to slice," she said, laying the piece on a plate and handing it to him with a knife for the butter. Laughing, she added, "There's no way to eat hot bread and butter with any kind of manners. Just butter it and ladle some compote on your plate and fall to. I believe I'll have some myself. Then I need to skip dinner. I'm getting so fleshy here of late."

Grateful for the inconsequential patter of the elderly woman, Matt buttered the hunk of fresh bread and took a bite. "Umm, that tastes wonderful. I've missed good hot yeast bread here of late. Lillie is frail, you know, and Flora does most of the cooking. She hasn't quite got her hand in on yeast bread. She makes good biscuits and cornbread, but I think she has even let her yeast starter die."

"Just tell her to mention it to me when she is ready to get started again. I'll give her some."

Matt finished his bread and drank a dipper of the cool water. "Mrs. Goodgion," he said, "I thank you for this delicious repast but I need to be on my way. I have an appointment with the undertaker in Chagris. Let me say, I'm glad to hear you've sent for your husband because I want him to preach my boy's funeral." He had to stop and swallow the lump in his throat and blink away the tears that filled his eyes. When he had regained his composure, he continued, "I don't know for sure when it will be but it will be as soon as possible. I can come back by on my way home and let you know."

"No, that won't be necessary. We'll come over there as soon as he gets home. We both want to give what comfort we can to the family."

At the furniture store that included funeral furniture, Mr. Bryce's expertise as a funeral director bolstered Matt's sagging courage in a way that neither his visit to Mr. Pendleton nor to Mrs. Goodgion earlier that day had done. Not only did he suggest practical ideas for the services; he had men lined up to open the grave.

"I suggest we hold the funeral from your home at nine o'clock in the morning. That will give us time to open the grave tomorrow. Many people are superstitious about leaving a grave uncovered overnight. I'll bring your son home this afternoon. That should give your family a chance to have some privacy to mourn before your friends come to sit up with him tonight. How does that sound to you?"

Matt nodded his head in agreement. "If you'll figure it all up, I can pay you now. I went by the bank and got greenbacks for my cotton I sold yesterday."

On his way home, gloom descended on him and covered him like a shroud. Thoughts raced though his mind about the activities of the previous night from the time he had heard shots and found Paul's body until this morning when he learned of the defection of his eldest son. Events seemed to refuse to follow timely procession but fell pell-mell over one another until he became confused about which had happened first. He kept coming back to Buford's departure and the circumstances that precipitated it. I followed every principle I believe in to raise that boy right and failed miserably, he thought. I'm responsible for Paul's death, too. If I had only forced Buford to face the authorities in Texas instead of running off up here, Paul would still be alive.

He dreaded facing Lillie and their children when he reached home. None of the children had experienced the loss of a close family member before and the present situation could only intensify their horror and grief. Lillie's reaction could be predicted by the way that she had collapsed after Terence's passing.

Matt's emotions were in such turmoil by the time he reached home that he didn't want to see anyone but his own family. He bypassed the entry from the new road and rode on to the crude path they had hacked out the previous winter. But when he topped the rise and saw the cotton fields overflowing with neighbors come to harvest his crop, the hard knot within him broke and a flood of grief engulfed him. He laid his head on the horse's neck and let the tears flow.

While he unsaddled his mount and led him to water Betsy ran from the house and wrapped her arms around his legs. He stooped and picked her up and hugged her. His heartache eased a little as he felt the warmth of the small body in his arms. His other children came to him from the field, Plez accompanying Flora to the edge of the field. Matt's anger burned hot when he saw Plez take Flora's hand and speak earnestly to her as they parted.

Speaking to her in front of all her brothers and sisters, Matt said, "I told you not to have anything to do with that Indian. It looks to me like you haven't paid any attention. I'll tell you again. I don't want to see him around here or hear of the two of you meeting any place else." He fixed his gaze on each of his children in turn until he knew he had their attention. "I mean this. I expect every one of you to uphold me and not aid or abet them in any way."

The six of them stood still and silent until Flora turned and ran sobbing into the house. Ida tried to follow her but Flora waved her off.

Betsy wiggled in Matt's arms and he set her down. "We'd better go see about your Ma," Matt told the others.

CHAPTER 12

Lillie

That morning Lillie Conover had lain in bed staring upward with eyes that had seen no sleep. Early morning light from the south and west windows played across the unpainted beaded ceiling. At this time of year, the sun had begun its journey to the Southern Hemisphere and its daily course bisected the house at the peak of the roof. Air coming in through the open windows had become cooler during the night and she reached for the light coverlet at the foot of the bed and pulled it up over her.

She heard sounds from the front room that she identified as dishes being cleared from the breakfast table and dumped into the gray enamel dishpan. Ida and Flora chattered at the job, but Lillie could not make out any words. When one of the girls poured water from the teakettle over the dishes, she could almost feel the steam rise to cover her face.

She heard Ida say, "Let's let the dishes soak for awhile."

Lillie's aching heart eased a little at Flora's exasperated tone as she replied, "No, we'll leave a clean kitchen when we go to the field." Then, softly, "And keep your voice down. Ma is trying to sleep."

At least two of my children are behaving normally, Lillie thought. Her heartache returned in full force as she remembered the night just passed and the two of her children whose lives had taken such an abnormal turn.

When she heard the shots, she had been in the process of cutting cakes into serving slices. Halfway through a slice, she had stopped dead still as a cold foreboding gripped her. Silly, she told herself, you always expect the worst when one of your children is out of your sight. Finishing the slice, she pulled the knife out of the cake and cleaned the icing from it with her fingers before laying it down. She licked her fingers and wiped them on a corner of her apron.

Every small detail seemed etched in her consciousness. As she remembered joining the knot of women who huddled together in the kitchen, she had looked through the door into the other rooms at the girls and women left stranded when all the men had gone to find out the reason for the shots. Flora and Esther held hands and whispered to each other.

She saw Ida join them and heard her say, "I'm going down there and find out for myself what's going on."

Flora grabbed her arm as she started to leave, saying, "No, you're not. It's no place for a woman."

Lillie saw Ida's temper flare. She jerked away from her sister and headed for the door. Lillie stepped to the doorway and said, "Ida, I want you to do something for me. Go see if you can find Holt and Betsy and bring them to me. I think several of the bigger boys were told to corral the littler ones and keep them here, but you know Holt. He may have squirmed his way out of their sight."

Ida soon returned with both Holt and Betsy in tow. Lillie gathered her children around her and said, "It's probably nothing to concern us, but it may break up the party. So I think I'll talk to the other ladies and see if we can go ahead with serving."

She went into the kitchen, talked with the other ladies, and came back, saying, "We decided to serve the younger ones now and wait until the men come back to serve the rest of us. Holt, you go and get the ones in the yard so they can get washed up. We'll set lamps in the windows so all of you can see to eat on the porches. Find a place and the girls will bring your plates and bowls out to you."

The flurry of activity broke the tension. Soon everyone's spirits seemed to lighten as they scooped ice cream and placed it and slices of cake onto plates, saucers, or bowls. All the children had been served and their serving dishes returned to the kitchen. Lillie dried dishes as Judith McMasters handed them to her from the scalding water.

She saw Plez quietly open a door into the dining room and meet Flora as she ran to him. He spoke softly to her. The color drained from her face and Plez caught her as she fainted. Lillie dropped the saucer, heard it shatter on the floor, and hurried to her daughter. She began chafing Flora's wrists and realized someone, she knew not who, had replaced her and someone else lifted her to her feet. Judith McMasters knelt and washed Flora's face with a cloth until she stirred and sat up.

Lillie turned to Plez then. She didn't have to ask. He said in a tightly controlled voice, "Mrs. Conover, it's Paul. Someone ambushed him. All of us got there too late to help him." His voice broke then and he sobbed.

Lillie put her arms around him. He's just a boy, she thought. Over the past few months, Plez and Paul had become fast friends. It's funny, she thought, Matt had no objection to their friendship despite his unyielding disapproval of any association between Flora and Plez. Any fool can see that they're in love, she thought. Maybe Matt can see it, too, and that's the reason he's so stubborn.

Lillie's children surrounded her with Flora and Plez standing hand in hand. Polly joined their group and put her arm around Ida. Astounded at how calm she felt, Lillie directed her family as they gathered their belongings.

Prudence Goodgion said, "You might as well have what's left of the cakes you brought. I have them fixed so you can take them home. Is there anything else?"

"Thank you, Mrs. Goodgion," Lillie said, "There's a box behind the wood box in the kitchen. It contains presents for my girls' birthdays—Flora and Ida's. My husband picked it up in town today when he went to the gin." Was that today? It felt like years ago. Matt, she thought suddenly, Matt doesn't know.

She caught Plez' attention. "Someone will have to go to our place and tell Matt. We left him a note. I can't imagine..."

Plez stopped her. "Mr. Conover is the one who reached Paul first. He has taken over and is trying to handle matters. He sent after the deputy. I think he wants you all to stay here until he sends after you. It happened within sight of the main road and he'd rather you didn't come by at this time."

Time dragged while they waited for further news. Lillie's senses felt honed to their sharpest edge as she noticed every little detail of the scene around her. The ladies had brought chairs and insisted she and her family sit in them. It seemed the polite thing to do, but Lillie needed to pace the floor. However, Betsy had climbed into her lap. She hugged the child to her and rocked in the swaying motion common to mothers the world over. Ida chewed on a fingernail, a habit she was trying to break. Rebuke rose to Lillie's lips; she stifled it. Flora gripped Plez' hand as if lifeblood flowed between them. I think it does, Lillie thought. Holt knelt on one knee tossing a rock back and forth from one hand to the other. He dropped it and it rolled away from him. Without rising from his kneeling position, he stretched his body and arm until he retrieved the stone and resumed pitching it. His agility and dexterity surprised Lillie. I haven't been paying enough attention to him, she thought.

Ben's arrival found Lillie and her family sitting in their wagon ready to go. A few of the men had straggled back and their retelling the tragedy had been more than she could take. For the sake of her children she had tried not to let her true feelings come to the surface. I don't know what my true feelings are, she thought, I don't feel anything. It can't be real; I'm having a nightmare. Every movement of her body required thought. Betsy climbed into her lap and she had to order her hands to leave her lap to give her room, instruct her arms to encircle the small child and hug her close when Betsy, crying aloud, snuggled against her breast. Holding her youngest melted the cake of ice that had seemed to form inside her and she muttered a soft hush, hush to the weeping child.

Betsy snubbed and dug her fist into her eyes; before they arrived home she slept deeply. Ben carried her inside and laid her on the front room bed.

"You might as well put her to bed in our room, Ben," Lillie told him. Ben picked her up and held her against his upper body where she flopped like a rag doll. He supported her head on his shoulder as he bore her from the room.

"She's all tuckered out," he said as he closed the door quietly behind him when he returned. "She'll sleep till morning."

"Ma, I'm going to build a fire in the cook stove and make a pot of coffee," Flora said. "I think we have enough beans roasted for one pot. I'll roast some more after the stove gets hot."

Lillie nodded assent; she didn't trust her voice just now. Realization of the tragedy came in waves and one had hit her with dreadful force as he saw Ben and Flora taking charge. My older children are growing up, she thought, but one will never grow old. Oh, Paul, Paul. Tears brimmed in her eyes and overflowed. She turned away and secured a handkerchief from her apron pocket. Dabbing at her eyes she swallowed her tears for the sake of her children.

Flora had a fire going in the range with the help of Ben's whittled shavings. Ida and Holt sat at the dining table as if made of wood. Lillie saw Holt's head droop and jerk as he roused from a momentary doze.

"Go over there and lie down, Holt," she said. "Pull your shoes off first."

Holt protested. "I want to wait until Pa gets here," he said.

Ben sat at the table beside him. "Then why don't you go pile up on the outside bed? That way you'll be the first to see Pa."

Holt agreed to the suggestion, and after hugging his mother goodnight, he left letting the screen door bang behind him.

Betsy stirred in the bed beside her mother and interrupted Lillie's replaying in her mind of the past night. Worn out from hard play all day and again at the party, the child had hardly moved all night. She and Matt had let her sleep with them rather than send her to her own bed in the room with her sisters.

Having an odd number of boys and girls makes sleeping arrangements difficult, she mused. They kept a bed set up in the front room to take care of the extra boy. Then the thought she had been trying to squelch struck her: I have an even number of boys now. She turned on her side and wept, pulling the pillow around her face to stifle the sobs.

After the fit of weeping, she rolled onto her back again. Betsy, without waking, snuggled against her and settled into tranquil slumber.

Lillie lapsed into her mental recitation of the previous night's events. It calmed me to remember the early part of the night, she thought, I don't know why. But I can't bear to think of my precious Matt's grief. I don't know what to make of the way Buford handled this, either.

After Ben left to go sit with Jed, the rest of the family had gone to bed. Sometime during the night Matt had drifted into an uneasy sleep but she remained wide-eyed. The restlessness she had felt ever since hearing the first shot returned in full force and she felt she could not tolerate another minute of inaction. She pulled up her knees slowly past Betsy's small figure lying halfway to the foot of the bed and put her feet on the floor. Checking to see that Matt had been undisturbed, she slid her feet into a pair of knitted house slippers, crossed the rag rug, and eased the bedroom door open. When the door made no noise, she blessed Matt for his diligence in keeping hinges oiled.

The front room had darkened with the setting of the moon but she knew every inch of it. However, someone could have left a dining chair out of place, she thought, as she felt her way around the table straightening each chair as she came to it. By the time she circled the table, her eyes had become accustomed to the darkness so that she crossed to a window without having to feel her way. Leaning her cheek against the cool glass, she listened to the ticking of the mantle clock she had inherited from Grandmother Thompson. She heard the whir it made before striking and counted three chords. Over two hours until first light, she thought, and decided to go outside to pace the yard.

Movement in the yard stopped her from leaving the window and she hunkered down to skylight the three figures silhouetted against a sky only slightly lighter than they were. She watched Buford cinch his saddle, check his bedroll, and pick up the reins. He stopped for a long look around the homestead then led his horse down the lane toward the main road, the dog following.

Unsurprised, she stood at the window watching the lane long after Buford disappeared from sight then moved to her rocker and sat in it with her arms around her drawn-up knees and reflected on the last few years of Buford's life. Matt had no idea that she knew of Buford's trouble with the law that had driven them from Texas to this raw red land. She wondered sometimes how he thought she could leave her sisters as well as her loved ones buried in the Texas soil that had been her home for more than thirty years. Pa and Ma and my precious Terence, she thought, and her already heavy heart felt the weight of an old grief ready to spring to the surface whether bidden or not. She quashed the memory by forcing herself to concentrate on Buford. His transgression must be serious this time for him to skedaddle like that before Paul's funeral.

Paul's funeral. There is something useful I can do, she told herself. I'll get Paul's clothes ready. With Buford gone and Holt in the yard, the dugout was empty. Not wanting to soil the house slippers in the yard, she pulled them off and padded across the room with bare feet. I'm a pretty sight, she thought, dressed in nothing but my gown. But my shoes and clothes are in our bedroom and I don't want to disturb Matt.

She found matches in the cabinet and lighted the lamp. Leaving it on the dining table where it shed light on the whole room, she crossed to the corner where their better clothes hung protected from dust by patchwork quilts. Ordinarily she would have paused to admire the colorful patterns decorating a corner which otherwise would be drab, but intent on her purpose, she pushed the quilts aside and quickly found Paul's suit among the few garments. The ends of his favorite black string tie dangled from the coat's breast pocket. Laying the garment across her arm, she picked up the lamp and made her way to the dugout.

Setting the lamp on the makeshift table beside the bed, she surveyed the room, seeing it for the first time since she had moved out of it into the house. The room was only slightly larger than the space required for two beds separated by a narrow walkway the width of the table. One of the beds had been moved to the yard for the summer and a tub filled with dirty clothes sat in its place. The trunk Matt had inherited from his mother filled the corner at the foot of the remaining bed. The lid was open and the clothes in it were disarranged; Buford must have rummaged through it and thrown part of the clothes on the bed. The bed had been left unmade and the general untidiness of the area energized Lillie to action.

She took all the clothes out of the trunk hunting for the shirt she wanted. All her four older boys were near enough the same size that they swapped clothes until she hardly knew what belonged to which. Folding each shirt neatly, she replaced them in the trunk. She found a clean pair of socks but not the shirt she wanted. Glancing at the tub of dirty clothes, she saw a sleeve of the shirt hanging over the side. Shoot, she thought, we'll have to do it up. Stepping on the rag rug running beside the bed, she made the bed and laid the suit, string tie, and socks in a neat pile on it. Then she gathered up the dirty shirt and, carrying the lamp carefully, maneuvered through the tricky inward-opening screen door of the dugout and the outward-opening door of the house.

The clock had stuck four before she returned to bed to lie sleepless and mull over the previous night's occurrences until she finally believed they had truly happened.

Recalling the need to launder the shirt prodded her to action. She jumped up from the bed waking Betsy. "Time to get up," she told the child. "We've got lots of work to do today."

Betsy's lips trembled and the corners of her mouth pulled downward. "I don't want to pick cotton today."

"Now, don't tune up to bawl. We'll go get us some breakfast and we'll both feel better. Come on, now, get dressed." Lillie pulled her own dress over her head and reached for her shoes. "Hurry up, you're a big girl; you know how to dress yourself."

Flora came to her when she entered the kitchen and hugged her. "I sent Ida on to the field. You won't believe it. All the neighbors showed up soon after daylight and they have the cotton patch covered."

Lillie could easily believe it. Help of neighbors in time of need had often determined whether a frontier settlement succeeded or failed. Indian Territory had been settled since before the Civil War but many of the white settlers looked on it as a frontier. She looked for the shirt she had laid across the back of a chair and spied it in a dishpan of boiling water on the stove.

"Ma, I dabbled the shirt out. Is that all right? I thought boiling it would make it white enough." Flora said. "It's about ready to wring out and starch. Do you think we'll have time for it to dry?"

"Hang it out while Betsy and I eat breakfast. Maybe it will be dry enough to iron. If not, I'll have to iron it dry."

"I'll iron it, Ma," Flora said.

"No, I want to do it myself." It's the last thing I'll ever get to do for Paul, she thought, as tears spilled down her cheeks.

Flora lifted the pan of boiling water and carried it outside to rinse the shirt and hang it to dry. Lillie dried her eyes on the wadded-up handkerchief from her pocket. She filled two plates with food from the warming oven, poured a cup of coffee, and called Betsy to breakfast.

CHAPTER 13

Matt

Matt didn't know what to expect when he saw Lillie again that morning. When he slipped out of bed before daylight, she had pretended to be asleep. It was a device she used when she didn't want to face him for some reason. He wondered if she thought he couldn't tell the difference between real sleep and fake. But, even so, he preferred to see her alone. He expected that Flora had shut herself in her room so would pose no problem but he sent the other children back to the field.

Betsy demurred. "Ma said I didn't have to pick cotton today," she whined.

He said, "Go with Ida. You don't have to pick but stay with Ida and don't bother any of the neighbors."

Once they were gone, he trudged to the back door and let himself in. The smell of freshly brewed coffee greeted him as he closed the door. Mingled with it, the odor of fresh-washed wood caused him to look at the floor still wet from a scrubbing of lye soap. He stretched forward until he hooked a ladder-back chair and dragged it to him. Sitting there, he wrestled his boots off and set them on top of the wood box. He still had not seen Lillie.

In his stocking feet, he padded to the cabinet for a cup and saucer and poured coffee. Sitting at the table, he took a spoon from the spoon holder in the center of the table and tasted cream from the cream pitcher. Finding it still sweet, he poured a small amount into his cup, then tipped coffee into the saucer, blew it to cool it, and, holding the saucer in both hands, brought it to his lips. Over the rim of the saucer, he saw Lillie pull back a fold of the quilt hanging across the room's corner and stick her head out.

"I've mopped myself into a corner again," she said.

She sounded so much like a child that he laughed. "Leave your shoes there and come have a cup of coffee," he said. "See, I'm in my stocking feet."

He got up, fetched a cup and saucer and poured coffee for her. She sat at the table and picked the cup up with both hands and brought it to her lips. He always wondered how she could drink scalding coffee without getting burned, but she insisted that she liked it that way.

"When did you start waiting on me?" she said.

"I've always waited on you. Are you just now noticing that?"

She reached out her hand and patted the back of his big one, which seemed to turn over of its own volition to squeeze hers. They sat thus, holding hands silently and finished their coffee.

Lillie said, "Do you want any more coffee?"

Matt shook his head. Looking around the room, he saw that it had been prepared for the funeral.

"I had Ben and Flora help me and we took down the bed," Lillie said. "That should give us room for chairs and benches for people to sit. We can push the table against the wall to give more room. I thought we could place the coffin in front of the quilt. What do you think?"

Relieved that Lillie seemed to have taken charge, Matt agreed to her plans. "Mr. Bryce said he'd bring Paul home today and to plan the funeral for nine o'clock in the morning," he said. "I talked to

Mrs. Goodgion and she said they will come over when he gets home today. Do you think you are up to talking to them?"

"Yes, of course." Lillie appeared surprised at the question. "What's wrong with Flora? She came running in here and slammed the door to her room. I thought I'd leave her alone a little while to get it out of her system and then go talk to her."

"I put my foot down about her and that Indian boy and hurt her feelings. She'll get over it."

Lillie turned from the cabinet where she had been washing their few dishes and came back to sit in her chair. She laid her arms on the table and laced her fingers together. Not lifting her gaze from her hands, she said in a slow voice, "No, Matt, I don't think she will. I don't believe you have faced it, but she is head over heels in love with Plez. And he feels the same way about her. No, I don't think she'll get over it."

Matt felt anger rising like bile in his throat. "Blast it, Lillie, you know why I hate Indians. My own brother died in my arms during the uprising in seventy-three. I saw the savagery in their faces and heard it in their blood-curdling yells. It's been more than thirty years and I still dream about it sometimes. I won't have one of them in my own family. It turns my stomach to think of it. Do you actually think I could dandle a Redskin on my knee and call it my grandchild?"

Flora flung the bedroom door open and stormed out to the table opposite him. Leaning on it with both hands, she thrust her face near her father's and said, "You say Redskin like you're spitting out a chew of tobacco. I lie awake at night and dream of having Plez' children. You make them sound like bastards."

Lillie caught Matt's arm when he drew back to slap her. "Don't, Matt," she said. "We've got enough trouble today. Don't make it any worse."

Matt felt the white hot temper cool to a steady flame. Never before had he raised a hand to this daughter. All the other children, even Betsy, had felt his switching and paddling, but Flora had never needed physical discipline. He could always talk to her. He tried it now.

"Don't ever let me hear you say that word again," he said.

Flora stared at him with the same baleful look and kept her face inches from his.

"I mean it, young lady. As long as you live under my roof, you'll keep a civil tongue in your head. I'm surprised you ever heard such a vulgar word let alone spoke it."

Flora closed her eyes and he saw a teardrop seep from under her eyelids and hang on her dark lashes. Good, he thought, her temper is cooling.

In a gentle voice, he said, "I reckon if you heard what your Ma and I were saying, you know why I feel the way I do."

Flora straightened up, pulled out a chair, and sat. Tears filled her eyes and she pulled a handkerchief from her pocket and wiped them. "I'm sorry I let my temper get away from me," she said. "I've heard the story about Uncle Paul all my life. I know this thing with Brother Paul brings it all back. But it hurts me, too." She broke down and buried her face in her hands.

Matt pushed back his chair, scraping it across the floor. He rounded the end of the table, pulled her to her feet and took her in his arms. While she sobbed against his shoulder, he looked across at Lillie. Although she, too, cried softly, she seemed to be taking it better than he expected.

He smoothed Flora's hair and murmured, "Hush, hush."

Flora backed out of his arms and wiped her eyes. "There," she said, "I guess I've got my cry out." She hesitated and Matt knew she had more to say. He waited and finally she said, "Pa, there's something I have to ask. I promised Plez. He wants to be one of the men who sit up with Paul's body tonight."

"No!" The word burst from Matt's lips without thought. Seeing the stricken look on Flora's face, he wished he could call it back. I can't change my feelings at the drop of a hat, he thought, but maybe

I can soften it a little. "Not tonight. This is too soon for me. I'll have to think about it longer than that."

Flora tried again. "You don't seem to realize the difference in savage Indians and Plez. These tribes here are civilized. That's what they call them—the civilized tribes. Plez was brought up to be gentle. He even has more schooling than I do. I wish you'd get to know Plez, Pa, you'd see how sweet he is."

A knock on the front door surprised Matt. Usually he heard any commotion of arrival. On his way to answer the knock, he said to Flora, "We'll have to talk about this later."

Mr. and Mrs. Goodgion stood before the door, both of them laden down with food. Matt pushed the screen door open for them to enter.

Mrs. Goodgion said, "I brought three loaves of hot bread and a pot of chicken and dumplings. Good afternoon, Lillie, Flora, where shall I put this?"

Before Lillie had a chance to answer, the back door opened and all the rest of Matt's children burst in. Betsy ran to Mrs. Goodgion for a hug. Flora took the pan of bread from her and set it on the stove away from the hottest burners.

Mr. Goodgion drew Matt away from the general hubbub to discuss plans for the funeral but all three boys followed them. I've taught them better manners than this, Matt thought. He turned toward them with a scowl.

Before he could say anything, Ben spoke. "Pa, both wagons are full and all the neighbors have gone home. Jed and I thought we might could take them to the gin in Chagris. Is that all right?"

"What time is it? Midafternoon?" Matt looked at the clock on the mantle. "Earlier than I thought. Yes, we might as well give it a try. You may have to come home in the dark. Have you had anything to eat?"

"Yes, Pa, we had dinner before you got back. We'd like to take some of Mrs. Goodgion's bread and a jar of milk. That should be plenty for supper."

Jed said, "Holt wants to go with us, okay?"

Betsy overheard and ran to her father. "Me, too. I want to go."

Holt pushed her away. "This is man's work. You can't go."

"Holt is right this time, Little Bit. You stay with Ma and the girls. But Holt can't go either. We'll need him to milk with Jed gone."

CHAPTER 14

Jed

Jed tried to wake up by shaking his head from side to side but failed. He felt tangled in heavy quilts and tried to push with his legs but they must have become paralyzed. He called to Ben but his mouth wouldn't open and the only noise he could make reminded him of a small animal's mewling. Then his shoulder shook violently and he opened his eyes to see Ben hovering over him.

"Wake up, Little Brother, you're having a bad dream. It's time to get up. Pa called us fifteen minutes ago."

Jed forced his eyelids open again and blinked. "It's still dark. What time is it?"

"What's the matter? You've never seen the sun rise? We have lots to do before nine o'clock. It'll take all hands and then some. Come on, now, on your feet before I pour water on your face."

Jed swung his feet to the rag rug covering the hard packed dirt floor between the beds, put on his overalls, and scratched around until he found his shoes. He pulled on socks and stuck his feet in the high top shoes, tightened the laces and, without tying the strings, followed Ben up the dugout steps. Light spilling from the kitchen window guided him to the wash stand near the back door. Ben stepped to one side to give Jed room at the wash basin and dried his face on the ducking towel hanging from a nail driven into the wall. Jed splashed his head and neck with the cold water and rubbed vigorously with the towel Ben handed him. He fumbled on the shelf for a comb and ran it through his hair.

"There," he said to Ben, "I feel like a human again. Let's see if Flora has fixed any breakfast."

Inside, they found the whole family assembled with the exception of Betsy. Their mother and the two girls dished up a hearty breakfast.

Matt said, "Come sit, boys. We're waiting to say grace."

Jed speared a slice of fried fatback and began cutting it up while he waited for the platter of eggs and the plate of hot biscuits to reach his place. When Holt passed the food to him, he raked three eggs onto his plate and added three biscuits.

As he broke the biscuits open and slathered butter on them, Matt said, "You boys are mighty hungry this morning. How did the cotton ginning go?"

Ben answered before Jed could speak. "They had quite a line waiting when we got there. I don't think they would have taken us under other circumstances. We finished up about dark and drove on back home. We tumbled into bed as soon as we got the teams fed and watered. Neither of us had been to bed in two days."

Flora had taken up another pan of hot biscuits. Jed grabbed two of them and buttered them while they were still hot. "Where are your manners?" his sister taunted.

"Now, Flora," Lillie said. "We agreed that we'd have no fussing today. Your brother isn't in his grave yet."

Flora ducked her head and said, "I'm sorry, Jed. I didn't mean it."

Jed turned in his chair and looked behind him toward the corner where Paul's coffin rested in front of the quilt that hung across the corner of the room. Another quilt covered the closed casket. He hadn't noticed it before; he had left with the wagonload of cotton before the undertaker brought it home. His throat constricted. He laid the biscuits on his plate and bolted for the door.

Greeted by the cool autumn air, he felt the queasiness of his stomach ease. He leaned against the wall, gulped a breath and blew it out slowly. The door opened and Flora came to him proffering a wet washcloth.

"Wash your face with that," she said. "You'll feel better. I truly am sorry I said what I did. Forgive me?"

He massaged his face with the soft cloth until his nausea subsided. Handing it back to her, he said, "Flossie, there's nothing to forgive. I thought you were teasing."

She put out her hands to him. He put both arms around her and brother and sister wept together as pinks and yellows glowed in the eastern sky and the day they dreaded dawned in pastel glory.

Grief spent for the moment, they returned to the kitchen. Lillie poured them hot coffee and they sat with the family to drink it.

Matt stood and said, "We need to get the morning chores over with before people starting arriving. Ida, you and Jed milk the cows like you usually do. Ben and Holt and I will tend to the rest of it." He stroked Lillie's hair. "Will you be all right? Flora will need help cleaning up and setting up the chairs and benches for the service. Where's Betsy? She can drag chairs and do her part."

From the scowl on her face, Jed thought his mother would make a sharp retort. But she only said, "I thought I'd let Betsy sleep a while longer. She'd just get in the way this morning."

She's taking her own advice, Jed thought. I'll watch my tongue, too. I spout off too much without thinking.

At the barn, Jed scooped feed into the trough for his first cow and pulled up a three-legged stool. He sloshed water on her udder and washed it, put the milk bucket between his knees, and pushed the top of his head into her right flank. "Saugh," he said to the cow after she kicked at him with her foot when he pushed it back out of his way.

Soon milk played a tune in the bucket as he alternately squeezed with one hand, then the other. Jed had milked twice a day for ten years; the procedure required no conscious thought. Today, though, he resisted contemplating his troubles. However, memories of Vinnie's announcement sneaked their way into his brain. In his mind's eye, he saw her earnest face, felt her hand on his arm, and heard the plea and shame in her voice as she said, "I'm with child."

He gripped his hands into fists and the cow kicked him. He turned loose of her teats to grab the milk bucket scarcely saving the milk from spilling. Setting the bucket a safe distance from her, he stroked and soothed her until she settled down. He tried to finish milking her, but she refused to give down her milk.

Ida stood, looked at him over the back of the cow she had been milking and said, "What's wrong with Bossy?"

"I accidentally pinched her and now she won't give down her milk." Jed felt like kicking her. *I feel like kicking anything that gets in my way,* he thought. *But that won't get the chores done.* "She's temperamental, anyhow. Do you want to change cows with me and see if you can do anything with her?"

"Give her another scoop of feed and see if you can't finish her." Ida sat and resumed her task. "And try to keep your mind on what you're doing."

Jed determined to follow her advice and concentrate on the job at hand. More feed worked wonders on Bossy's reluctance and milk soon filled the bucket. Jed released her into the lot and called Precious. Although she was Bossy's calf, her disposition differed entirely from that of her dam. She hurried into position before Jed could fill her feed trough. When he perched once more on the three-legged stool, she backed her leg ready to be milked.

Jed's thoughts turned once again to his dilemma. In the time since their conversation, he found he had come to believe that Vinnie really was pregnant and not just trying to trap him. He doubted, too, that any other man had fathered the child. On the other hand, he knew that he would never get over his love for Esther. *I cannot marry Vinnie,* he thought. *I have to think of some way out of it.*

The idea sprang fully formed into his head. Disgusted that he would even consider such an action, he pushed it away. But it returned again and again even though he resisted until it gained a foothold. *Marry Esther first.*

The rest of the morning passed faster than Jed expected. They had barely finished their outside chores when Mr. Goodgion and two of his sons arrived with a wagonload of benches brought from the meeting house. Mr. Goodgion, dressed for preaching, directed his sons and the men of the Conover family as they set up the benches outside the front door. Inside seating would be reserved for the immediate family and close friends with the overflow assigned makeshift pews outside but close enough to the door to be able to hear.

When they were finished, Matt told his boys, "Go get your clothes for the funeral. I'll check to see if your mother and the girls are ready; we'll clean up and change in the two bedrooms."

He invited Mr. Goodgion and his sons to enter the house and relax while the family readied itself for the funeral.

"Thank you," David Goodgion said, "we'll wait out here in case anyone comes while you are still getting ready. Mrs. Goodgion and our two daughters-in-law should be along any minute. Perhaps you should show me where to place the food they'll bring."

Jed headed for the corner that held their good clothes. He had to sidle behind Paul's coffin and felt again the anguish he had been trying to push aside all morning. An urge to run away almost overwhelmed him. That would solve all my problems, he thought. Buford had the right idea.

Ben must have sensed his agitation because he put an arm around him on one side and Holt on the other and squeezed their shoulders. "Buck up, Broncs," he said. "We have to be brave and help Pa and Ma and the girls get through this."

Through his tears Jed saw young Holt square his shoulders and stretch his back ramrod straight. Knowing he could do no less, Jed followed suit, wiped his tears, and lifted his chin. "Lead on, Captain," he said. "Your troops are ready."

Thinking back on it later, he remembered sketches of the rest of that day. When he heard the first words of *Safe in the Arms of Jesus*, he turned to the sound and saw Esther standing just inside the doorway with her family. Her clear soprano blended with the other voices of the McMasters family and filled the room. He felt his sorrow subside for the duration of the song, but remembered not one word of the sermon. Instead his thoughts turned to formulating a plan to persuade Esther to marry him.

He saw Mr. Bryce remove the quilt covering the coffin and lift the lid. His hands and knees began shaking and he felt weak all over. The strains of *Nearer, My God, to Thee* assailed his ears and he want to cover them to shut out the words. Mr. Bryce led those friends from outside around the family and in front of the coffin. Jed couldn't look; he bent with elbows on knees and covered his face with his hands. He knew the elbow in his ribs meant Ben wanted him to sit up and act like a man, but he shook his head and didn't look up until the only sound was the quiet sobbing of his mother. He looked around then to find that his family had been left alone.

He looked toward the corner and felt relieved to see the coffin closed and covered once again. Not knowing what to expect next, he turned to his father. All the color seemed to have drained from Matt's face and his head bobbed and jerked. Unnerved, Jed elbowed Ben and nodded toward Matt.

Ben cleared his throat and said, "Pa." Matt appeared not to have heard, so Ben spoke louder. "Pa, how long do we sit here?"

Matt shook his head as if to clear it and spoke with an effort. "When all the family is ready to proceed, we'll open the door and go out." He studied the face of each one in turn, then stood. Lillie put her hand in his and rose to her feet. As they walked solemnly to the door, the children fell in behind with Ben bringing up the rear.

He recollected little of the procession to the cemetery, but had a clear picture of Plez Wilson waiting at the gravesite. Surprised, he realized that he had not seen Plez at the funeral. He thought Plez must have taken Pa's warning to heart until later when he saw Plez and Flora walk apart from the other mourners. They engaged in earnest conversation for several minutes before they clasped hands and Plez departed.

At last the morning ended and the family along with the preacher sat at table to eat some of the abundant provisions brought by the neighbor women who had come to the funeral. Mrs. Goodgion gently pushed Flora into a seat and served the meal by herself. For such a large woman, she moved quickly and gracefully.

Jed's appetite astounded him. He had not expected to be able to eat a bite. A feeling of peace descended on him. He knew it would not last but for the time being he pushed sorrow and trouble from his thoughts and numbed his mind. It was good to get back into a routine and he actually looked forward to milking time and Bossy and Precious.

CHAPTER 15

Matt

Matt Conover had never needed an alarm clock in his life. Even if he wanted to wake up at a different time than his usual four in the morning, all he had to do was to tell himself the hour and his eyes opened wide awake. When he took one of his infrequent daytime naps, he set the number of minutes in his mind and never slept longer. On the morning after Paul's funeral, he woke up with an uneasy feeling of having overslept. His legs felt like lead and the dull headache that began during the walk to the cemetery had progressed down his neck and back. He lay waiting for the clock to strike the hour, dreading this day almost as much as he had shrunk from the previous one.

His apprehension grew as the minutes passed and the clock failed to strike. Lillie slept beside him curled in a ball. He slipped out of bed as quietly as he could so as not to disturb her. Picking up his clothes and shoes and turning the doorknob slowly, he tiptoed out of the room. Feeling his way to the table, he fumbled in his overall pocket until he found a match and lit the lamp. Both hands of the clock pointed to the same number. Twenty after, he thought, I have overslept.

Quickly pulling on his clothes, he walked barefoot to the door of the girls' bedroom and knocked lightly. Usually Flora came out immediately, hair combed and dressed for the day. Not this morning. She's tired, too, he thought. He knocked louder and called, "Flossie, time to get breakfast. We need to be in the field by daylight."

The door opened a crack and a sleepy-voiced Ida said, "Flora's not here, Pa."

It was the last thing he expected to hear. He pushed the door open, nearly hitting Ida who jumped back out of the way. Lamplight from the kitchen penetrated only a short distance into the dark room. Nevertheless he proceeded to the bed not knowing what good he imagined it would do. As the implication of Ida's words hit him, he whirled and asked Ida, "Where is she?"

The girl sensed his intense anger and bridled. This one always gave as good as she got. In a defiant tone, she said, "She ran off last night and married Plez Wilson."

Questions flooded his mind and he knew not which to ask first. Instead he said, "And you were a party to it."

"Yes, I was." She sounded proud of it.

He wanted to shake her but knew he could not because he needed her cooperation. One thing he knew for sure, he must go after Flora and bring her home. Ida had the information he needed. He said, "What time did she leave?"

"About two o'clock."

She didn't elaborate. He was going to have to drag every tidbit of knowledge of the episode out of her. "Where did they go?"

"I don't know."

This conversation was getting him no place. "I'm going after her," he said. "You'll have to cook breakfast. Get your clothes on."

Ida wailed, "But, Pa, I don't know how. I can't even build a fire in the cook stove."

Everything seemed to conspire to delay his pursuit. "Do the best you can. I'll send Ben to make the fire. And Holt can take your place milking the cows."

Jed watered and saddled his horse for him. He bubbled with excitement at the news of the elopement. "Pa, why don't you just let them go? The only couple that's more in love is Esther and me."

It was the wrong thing to say. Matt's temper boiled over. "Your sister." He stopped and breathed slowly to try to get hold of himself, but it was no use. "Your sister," he spat out, "is underage. She's still under my authority. I will not have that Indian in my family. I told her as much and she has chosen to disobey me. I won't have it, I tell you."

He mounted the horse, took the reins from Jed, and slapped the horse's flanks. He rode at a fast clip until he reached the Wilson place. Tying his animal to the hitching post, he tromped up the steps and rapped loudly at the front door.

Baxter Wilson demanded from just inside the door, "Who's there?"

"Matt Conover."

Wilson threw open the door and said, "Come in, Man. What are you doing out so early this morning?"

"I came after my daughter."

"What?"

"I came after my daughter."

"But Ida's not here." Wilson seemed confused.

"Not Ida. Flora."

Polly appeared in the dining room doorway hastily tying the sash of her robe. Her raven hair fell in a tangle around her face, and as she moved toward them, she caught it back with one hand.

"Mr. Conover," she said, "Plez and Flora are not either one here."

Her father cut in. "Plez isn't here? What's going on?"

She spoke to her father. "They left last night to go get married."

Wilson turned to Matt. "We'd better discuss this calmly. Come on back to the kitchen. Polly will make us some coffee. Have you had breakfast?"

Matt's anger began to cool. Obviously Baxter Wilson was as much in the dark about the situation as he was. The pair must have conspired with Ida and Polly to help them elope. Ida had furnished him with so few facts that he had no idea where to look for his daughter and her man. Husband? Perhaps Wilson would have better luck with his child.

Polly soon served them coffee and set about preparing breakfast. Matt itched to be on his way but saw no civil way of hurrying the girl. By the time Polly served fried ham, eggs, and hot biscuits, the kitchen clock chimed five o'clock. He suspected the girl of taking her time to give the defiant couple a chance to get farther ahead of him. Twice he started to leave, but stayed in his seat because he didn't know where to go.

Polly settled herself in her chair and Baxter started passing the food. Matt served his plate and folded his hands in his lap waiting for the blessing, but the Wilsons began at once to eat. One more strike against them, Matt thought.

But, after he chewed a bite of ham, his own manners asserted themselves. "This is good," he said. "How do you keep it so fresh this time of year?"

Baxter Wilson seemed pleased. "After we sugar cure our hams, I hang them in the ice house at the store. They keep their quality a lot longer. This is our last one, though. I'm ready for hog-killing weather."

He spoke to Polly. "Tell Mr. Conover what you know about the doings of last night. Don't leave out any part of it."

Polly laid her fork and knife carefully on her plate and looked directly into Matt's eyes. "They made up their minds at the cemetery yesterday. Flora asked Ida and me to help them and swore us to secrecy. Last night Plez packed his things in the buggy and hid it and his horse out of sight and earshot of this house. My part was to keep Pa occupied so he wouldn't suspect anything. It was sort of hard when I heard the rattle of the buggy as it left the yard so I started playing the piano really loud."

She turned toward her father and lowered her eyes. Softly, she said, "I'm sorry to deceive you, Pa, but I'm not sorry they ran away."

"Plez is a grown man, Polly," Baxter said. "Nothing I could have said would have had any effect on him."

But you could have warned me; Matt almost put his thought into words but restrained himself.

Baxter went on, "You know more than you have told. Spit it all out."

"I know a little bit more about their plans," Polly said. "Plez went to Healdton right after the funeral and bought the marriage license. I don't know what time they got away last night, but they planned to stop at the first place they came to after daylight and get married. They won't be back for a week because they intend to take the train in Ardmore and go on a wedding trip. They didn't tell anyone where they were going. And I don't know which road they took to Ardmore. With a lot of the section lines at least passable, they could have traveled many different roads."

Matt felt as if a door had slammed in his face. He glanced at the clock. Nearly four hours had passed since the young couple slipped away. He wondered if he had time to notify the sheriff's office to have them apprehended but dropped the idea. Even if they could be stopped in such a way, he shied away from making a public spectacle of them.

Polly offered him another cup of coffee. He added extra cream and drank from the cup. Both Baxter and Polly Wilson finished their meal in silence. Grateful for the quiet time to reflect, Matt realized all of his options had disappeared. He could still have the marriage annulled, but knew that he would not do so after they returned from a week of being man and wife.

He finished his coffee and rose. "Thank you, Miss Polly, for a most delicious repast." He bowed formally.

She smiled and ducked her head, embarrassed.

Matt turned to Baxter. "I do appreciate the food and the company. I thought when I came here that I would pursue our children until I found them and bring my daughter home. I've changed my mind. I must warn you, though, that I don't know what my actions will be when they return. I forbade Flora's having anything to do with your son and I know he knew how I felt. Right now I don't think I can welcome them into my home."

Baxter had risen from the table as soon as Matt stood. "I'm sorry you feel that way, but I understand it."

Matt started to proffer his hand to Baxter, but didn't know whether or not he would be rebuffed. He decided not to risk it. "I'm much obliged for your hospitality," he said. "I'd best be getting home. It's past daylight."

"Yes, it's time I left for the store, too," Baxter said as he walked Matt to the front door, retrieved his hat from the hatrack, and bid him goodbye.

Although the sun peeked over the horizon and he knew he should have been working in the cotton patch since first light, Matt let his horse walk on the way home. He needed to focus on a schedule for the harvest but his thoughts kept returning to all the events crammed into a period of less than three days. Once in his younger days he had seen a squirrel in a cage at a medicine show. A wheel dominated the center of the cage and the squirrel ran on it keeping it in a constant rotation. The squirrel sometimes jumped to the wire walls and clung there looking from side to side. At other times it ran around the floor seeking a way out. I feel like that squirrel, Matt thought, trapped. Paul's death, Buford's desertion, Flora's defiance chased one another through his mind like a squirrel on a nonstop wheel. Like the squirrel, he saw no way out, so he allowed himself to recall all the details of each event of the last few days.

When he reached the corner halfway between his farm and Wilson's, instead of proceeding forward he turned south toward the cemetery. He found Pendleton on his knees beside Paul's grave.

When the old man saw him, he placed one hand beside him on the ground and pushed himself upright. "Morning, Matt," he said. "It gets harder every day to get up when I'm down." He pulled his glove from his right hand and held it out.

Matt reached across the grave and shook hands. He looked down to see a mass of flowers covering the grave. Their friends had stripped their flower gardens to bring bouquets yesterday. However, Matt could see a number of fresh blooms among the fallen petals and faded blossoms.

Pendleton followed his gaze. "I picked a few fresh ones this morning and scattered them while the dew is still wet. I thought that if any of your family came back today it might be some consolation."

Tears clouded Matt's vision; he swallowed to keep them from spilling over. "I'm much obliged for your kindness," he said.

"You're more than welcome," Pendleton said. "I imagine my daughter has breakfast ready by now. I'll be getting on. Stay as long as you like. And feel free to bring any of your family at any time."

After the elderly man left, Matt checked the whereabouts of his horse and located him on the outskirts of the cemetery grazing on the dry grass. Feeling guilty about leaving his family to do all the work, he nevertheless seemed rooted to the spot beside his son's grave. He stood there and tried unsuccessfully to restrain his grief. Great sobs racked his body and he dropped to his knees. "Oh, Paul, Paul," he cried. "I failed you, my son. I failed you." Additional waves of sorrow overcame him and, unmindful of crushing the blanket of flowers, he fell across the grave and lay there until he had spent his grief.

Rising, he squinted at the sun and judged it to be about an hour high. Time to get home. He strode to the monument and washed his face at the pump he had noticed there. Whistling to his horse, he placed his foot in the stirrup and, on the second trial, managed to bring the other leg over the horse. Pendleton is right, he thought, it gets harder every year to get up when I'm down. Today I feel every one of my fifty-seven years.

CHAPTER 16

Lillie

Lillie felt the mattress give and heard the springs creak when Matt eased his big frame from their bed. Matt's clothing rustled when he picked it up and his shoes scraped slightly as he lifted them from the floor. The lock clicked before and after the door swung on its well-oiled hinges. No wonder he keeps it oiled, she thought. He slips out like this every morning.

Lillie had dozed fitfully the early part of the night. Raw nerves attuned every sense to its highest level. Her ears picked up the softest sound. She smelled the acrid odor of the chrysanthemums she had brought from the burying and laid on the dresser. Her dry mouth tasted salty from the tears she had swallowed, her eyes felt grainy and her head throbbed. She had counted twelve tones of the striking clock and lay with her open eyes staring at the moonlighted window until she heard the single toll an hour later. She must have slept then because she knew nothing until Matt awakened her.

Betsy stirred, whimpered softly, and turned over onto Lillie's legs. Lillie thought, Tonight she moves back to the other bedroom. She scooted over to Matt's pillow and pulled the child up in the bed. Burying her face in the pillow, she smelled the good masculine scent of her husband and thought she could go back to sleep.

Most mornings she stayed in bed until time for breakfast. Two months before Betsy was born, the doctor had warned her that she must lie flat of her back or risk losing the baby. Twelve-year-old Flora had taken to cooking as if she had been born to be a chef, enjoying the job, begging to do all the cooking even after her mother's enforced bed stay ended after Betsy's birth. With all the extra duties attending the new baby, Lillie had been grateful for Flora's help. Over the years, she had relinquished her place at the stove until the kitchen belonged more to Flora than it did to her. Sometimes she resented the rest of the family's assumption that she no longer wanted that place. It had felt good to her Tuesday afternoon to be baking birthday cakes, a skill beyond Flora's competence.

Her keen sense of hearing picked up a difference in the morning sounds of her family. She heard Matt call out at the door of the girls' bedroom, heard a sleepy-voiced Ida answer, felt the vibration of the back door slam. A short while later Ben's placid tones seemed to quiet Ida's excited spate.

Lillie wondered why she couldn't pick out Flora's voice. Probably puffed up over her Pa's putting his foot down about her and Plez. It was her way to clam up rather than spout off like Jed or Ida. But when she heard a horse speed out of the yard and Jed and Holt come in the house talking excitedly, Lillie could stand it no longer. She threw back the coverlet and, not stopping for shoes or robe, went to see what was going on.

Ben had made a fire in the range and was trying to talk Ida into making coffee.

"I don't know, I told you," Ida said. "I don't know how to grind the beans, or how much grounds to use, or anything." The pitch of her voice rose higher and higher until she wailed. "Let's just eat this cold chicken and some bread and butter. Pa wants us to be in the field at daylight."

Lillie interrupted. "Somebody tell me what's going on," she said.

Her children looked at each other as if they had been caught in some mischief.

"Ida, you tell me. Where's Flora?"

Ben laid the piece of wood he had been shaving into kindling on the table, folded his knife, and put it in his pocket. He took the two steps that separated him from Lillie and put both hands on her shoulders. "Ma," he said, "maybe you'd better sit down. It may be hard for you to take what Ida has to tell you."

Lillie looked from one worried face to the other. A smile flickered and died around her lips. "She's run off with Plez," she said. "Did your Pa go after her?"

Jed and Ida looked relieved but Ben's voice showed his concern as he said, "Are you sure you're all right?"

She took his hands from her shoulders and squeezed them. "Of course, I'm fine. It's your Pa we need to worry about. Now, if the stove is hot, I'll get some breakfast. You boys sit if you are washed up. Ida, you can help me. I'll show you what to do." She set about gathering the ingredients for breakfast. "We don't have enough eggs for breakfast. It looks like we forgot to bring them in yesterday afternoon. Holt, go check the nests and bring in what you find. Hurry, now, I'll need them pretty quick. One of you other boys go wake Betsy and tell her to get ready for breakfast."

She had Ida slice the leftover bread that Mrs. Goodgion had brought the day before and to toast it in the oven while she ground the beans and made coffee. When Holt returned with eggs, she fried them and lifted them onto a platter that she placed in the center of the table next to the cold fried chicken. Her family made short work of the quick breakfast.

As they rose from table, she asked, "Do each of you have your morning chores laid out so you can start picking as soon as it's light enough?"

Holt said, "Pa told me to take over Ida's job of milking."

"Good. Then Ida can stay here and help me get the house work done." She saw Ida's frown. "I know, Missy, you'd rather work outside, but it's time you learned what needs to be done in the house. I plan to teach you to cook, too."

Ida said, "But what if Pa brings Flora back?"

Lillie doubted there was little chance, but she didn't want to tell her children that. Matt hadn't handled Paul's death and Buford's departure well at all. He hadn't said much but she knew him so well that she knew he was in turmoil inside. He hadn't talked with her about his worries for years, but she figured he told Jed things that he didn't mind having others know. Jed couldn't keep a secret. Ben, on the other hand, kept his mouth shut and Matt discussed serious matters with him. The problems of the last few days, though, affected every member of the family in a bad way. Matt would not want to add to the burden each youngster carried. Their first experience with the death of a close family member compelled them to find a way to deal with it.

Apparently Flora needed help from the man she loved in order to stand her grief. Lillie understood that even though she and Matt had failed to turn to each other. I hope Matt doesn't find her and bring her home, she thought. We need to give her and Plez a chance to depend on each other. To Ida, she said, "Even if he does bring her back, I am going to take my place in the kitchen. And, like I said, you need to learn things you'll need when you get married."

The two of them had washed dishes and strained and stored the morning's milk by the time daylight came. Lillie sent Ida and a protesting Betsy to the cotton patch while she remained in the house to complete the housework.

The sun had made inroads into its climb in the morning sky when she saw Matt ride into the yard. She had kept the coffee hot and grease in the skillet to prepare his breakfast but, after he unsaddled his horse and turned him in the pasture, he got his cotton sack and joined the children in the field. She didn't see him face to face until after she shook the cowbell to call them for dinner.

After a long morning's work in the field, the family attacked the noon meal Lillie had prepared. She had boiled dried butter beans and opened a half-gallon jar of hominy, picked tomatoes and okra in the fall garden and fried the okra, made a big pan of cornbread, and opened a jar of bread-and-butter pickles. Goblets of fresh sweet milk and the last of the birthday cakes completed the meal.

Her family had a habit of eating a meal without saying a word. She had finally gotten used to it after having been raised in a family that enjoyed a lively conversation at table. But today's silence punctuated only by the faint click of eating utensils on plates irritated her. "Matt," she said. When she had his attention, she continued, "Tell me what happened to Flora."

His face reddened. "She's gone." The words came out clipped.

She thought he would say no more, but he looked from one startled face to another and said in a tone that brooked no argument, "That's the last time I want her name mentioned in this house."

Betsy left her cake and milk to stand beside her mother. Lillie put her arm around her. She's never seen her father like this, she thought. For that matter, neither have any of the other children, at least not this bad. She tried to reason with Matt. "You're frightening the children," she began.

Matt laid his napkin beside his plate and pushed his chair back so suddenly that it fell over backward. He appeared not to notice. Jed rushed to right the chair.

Matt said, "I mean what I say. Now, it's time to get back to work." He headed out the door, all the children but Betsy following.

Lillie called Ben and Ida back. "Ida, you take Betsy and look after her this afternoon. Ben, hitch up the trap for me. I'm going to deliver all these dishes the neighbors brought. They'll be needing them. Besides, I want to thank each one personally."

She could tell Ida wanted to argue. She looked her in the eye and slowly moved her head from side to side one time. Her children didn't realize that she knew their term for the gesture: *that look*. Ida held her tongue and pulled Betsy from the room.

Ben said, "I'll hitch my horse, Ma." He walked back to her and kissed her on the cheek. "He's gentle, but you be careful."

Lillie hastily cleaned up the kitchen, hung her apron on a peg attached to the outside kitchen door, washed her face, and redded her hair. It took two trips to load all the dishes and she hoped to get home in time to pick black-eyed peas for supper and churn the butter. I may have to put Betsy on the churning, she thought.

First she visited Judith McMasters who lived a mile west of them across the road from the Wilson allotment. Judith was in the field with her family picking cotton, but she carried her sack to the scales, wiped her hands on her apron, and invited Lillie to sit and visit.

"No, I don't have time if I get all these dishes delivered today," Lillie passed Judith's dishes to her and climbed back up to her seat. "There are so many of them. All the neighbors have been so good to us. But I don't know how to find some of them. I thought you might be able to tell me. Haven't you lived here a long time?"

"Yes, we moved to the Chickasaw Nation in ninety-two. The first year we lived on the Washita, but I insisted Everett find us a better place the next year. We didn't have any water to use but that red Washita and it ruined all our clothes. You can't *get* that stain out. So he found the place we're on here and we've been here ever since. We like it here; the only drawback is the lack of education for the white children. I can read and write myself, but I'm no teacher. Esther is so excited that Jed is teaching her to read and write. She hasn't told any of the family but me. Has Jed told you?"

"No, I don't know a thing about it."

"They want to keep it secret until she gets really good at it, I guess. Land's sakes, *look* at us. We've gotten entirely off the subject. Tell me who you want to find."

Lillie produced the list she had made. As she read the names, Judith gave her directions to each place.

"Thank you," Lillie said. "I knew you were just the one to ask. I'll be on my way. Come to see us."

Delivering the dishes turned out to be more time consuming than Lillie had expected. Many of the houses sat back from the road; she had to tie the horse and carry the dishes down a lane to two of them. Except for the homes including elderly members who were too infirm to do hard work, she found most of the women in the field. She knew she had inconvenienced them but courtesy required return of the pans, platters, and plates at the earliest opportunity. One never knew how badly the utensil was needed.

At the last stop on that end of her route, Lillie pulled up to the hitching ring and walked down the two steps provided by the owners. Prudence Goodgion hurried from the meetinghouse that sat next door to her residence. Lillie stooped to loop the horse's tether in the ring.

"Come in, come in," the old lady said, tucking stray hairs in the knot on the back of her head.

"Thank you, Sister Goodgion. I brought back your bread pans and this huge platter. I thought you might need them."

"I wish you'd call me Prudence, Lillie. Yes, I do need the pans, but I seldom use that big platter. Or should I say charger? I think it's about the size of the one that carried John the Baptist's head. But that's another subject. Come sit on the porch and rest a spell. I'll draw a fresh bucket of water and we can have a cool drink."

Lillie settled into one of the rockers beside a wicker table. It was the first time she had stopped by the preacher's home. In fact, she had not been to church in the year they had lived in the area. Flora attended regularly and Ida had taken to going since she and Polly Wilson had become good friends. Jed went to every service because he knew Esther never missed. But she and Matt just hadn't gotten started. He still called for family devotions occasionally but they had slacked off in the past year. Paul's death had left emptiness in her heart that cried out for spiritual filling. But today she wanted help in absorbing the fact of Flora's elopement.

Prudence appeared around the corner of the house carrying a bucket and set it on the wicker table. "I'll just get us some glasses," she said as she disappeared through the screen door.

Lillie drank deeply of the water. "I didn't realize how dry I was," she said. "Thank you."

Prudence filled her glass again with the dipper. She reached into the basket beside her chair, picked out a sock, and proceeded to darn it. "You don't mind if I work while we talk, do you? I never seem to get caught up. Now that the boys are married, I try to help their wives with little things like this that I can just bring home with me." She worked in silence until she came to the end of the thread in the needle, lifted the sock to her teeth and bit off the thread. She rethreaded the needle, bit off the thread from the spool, rolled a knot in the end of the thread, and began filling the hole in a sock. "Now," she said, "tell me how you're doing."

Lillie didn't know how to start. She looked at her hands clasped in her lap as she said, "I have something I want to talk to somebody about, but it's not about Paul."

Prudence dropped the sock to her lap and laid her hand on Lillie's knee. "Did the young folks get away last night?"

Startled, Lillie looked into the kindly face of the old woman. "How did you know?"

"Plez came by here late yesterday afternoon to see if Mr. Goodgion would marry them, but he had already gone back to Reck. I tried to talk to him, but it was plain to me that he had his mind made up. He said he had the license and nothing or nobody was going to stop them. I wanted to warn you, but it was getting close to dark. My boys always check on me and do my chores night and morning, but they had already gone home by the time Plez came by. There was nothing I could do."

Lillie clenched her hands into fists, then relaxed them and clasped them in her lap. Swallowing the lump in her throat, she said, "I hate to burden you with this, but I don't know where else to turn."

"There, there, dear, that's what I'm here for."

The kind words brought tears to Lillie's eyes. "I feel I must ask you not to tell anyone about this visit, especially Flora."

"Mr. Goodgion and I have kept the secrets of many people over the years. Would it be all right if I tell him? He often has good ideas and you can trust him to keep mum."

A sense of relief settled in Lillie and she relaxed. I've come to the right person, she thought. "Prudence," she began, "my husband has laid the law down." She could go no further. Tears filled her throat choking back her words.

Prudence dipped water from the pail and refilled Lillie's glass. While she drank, the good lady said, "Matt and I had a nice visit the other day when he stopped by. He's a good man."

Lillie set the half-empty glass on the table. "I know he is, but he hasn't been himself since Paul was killed." She picked the glass up and sipped. "He has told the family that he doesn't even want to—." Tears slipped from her closed eyes and she fumbled in her sleeve for a handkerchief and wiped them. Taking another sip of water, she said, "He doesn't want to hear her name mentioned in our house."

A look of grave concern filled Prudence's brown eyes but she said nothing. She waited until Lillie found the courage to go on.

"I won't disobey my husband." Lillie lifted her chin a fraction and moistened her lips. "But a young bride needs her mother."

Prudence waited a minute before she broke the silence. "What do you want me to do?"

Lillie felt free to unburden her heart to the kind woman. I've found a real friend, she thought. "I've thought about it all morning. I guess I want you to take my place and befriend her without letting her know I asked. I never did meet Plez's mother, but she is gone now, anyway. I think Judith McMasters will do what she can, but I just don't feel free to ask her. You'll see Flora at church. I'm going to start myself this coming Sunday morning. She'll be gone this week, so I can start without causing a stir."

Prudence nodded and said, "Good. We'll be glad to have you. I hope Matt will come with you."

Lillie shook her head. "I doubt it. He's in such a state the last few days. But I'll be there." She rose to go. "I've lingered longer than I intended so I need to get back home. As it is, I'll have to wait until tomorrow to deliver dishes to the neighbors east of us."

"I appreciate your confidence in me," Prudence said as she enfolded Lillie in her arms. "I'll ask Flora to come over and help me bake bread. That takes several hours. Maybe we'll get a chance to talk. Oh, wait a minute; let me get you some starter to take home with you. Matt told me he thought Flora had let yours run out."

CHAPTER 17

Jed

Jed jumped up from the breakfast table the next morning before the rest of the family had half finished. He had bolted his meal to hasten his departure to town. "I want to get in line at the gin early to keep from getting wet. I think I smell rain."

Ben grinned and said, "Would you folks like me to translate that remark for you? It means he has a Saturday night date."

Ida said, "Or wants to stop by McMasters place on the way back and see his sweetheart." She eyed Jed with that devilish look she wore so often these days. "Oh, I forgot. It's the Wade place, isn't it?"

Jed felt the hot flush burn his back and tighten his neck. He knew his face almost glowed in the dim light cast by the lamp. "One of these days," he said to her, "I'm going to choke you."

"Children, children," Lillie said. "Both of you. You're nearly grown and still act like children."

Matt said, "What's this about Wade?"

Ida jumped in before anyone else had a chance. "Vinnie Wade asked him to dance with her at the party the other night and then they left together and didn't come back."

His father's deep-set blue eyes looked more like steel when he turned them on Jed. They're boring a hole right through me, Jed thought.

"When did you start having anything to do with that Wade bunch?" Jed couldn't think of a quick answer but apparently his Pa didn't expect one for he went right on. "Sometimes I don't think you have the sense you were born with. I've always taught all my children to pick the right companions. Those people are not our kind." He looked Jed square in the eye before he turned his gaze upon the wall opposite him. "Go on and take the cotton," he said. "But we'll have a talk when you get back." Jed was glad to escape. He grabbed his hat from the peg by the back door and made a hasty exit, remembering not to slam the door behind him. No use in riling Pa any more than he already had. I'm getting it from all sides, he thought.

He was second in line at the gin in Chagris. Judging the wagon ahead of him to be half-emptied, he knew he had barely time to pen the note asking Esther to meet him at their trysting place soon after moonrise. Before he left home he had filched a page from his mother's letter writing tablet and grinned as he imagined her saying, "They're not putting as much paper in these tablets as they used to."

Fishing his pocketknife and a stub of pencil from his overall pocket, he whittled the lead in the pencil to a point and began his note. He had to be careful to choose words that Esther could decipher. Even though he had only a sixth-grade education, he hadn't yet taught her to that level. But it wouldn't be long at the rate she learned. She had a quick mind and sometimes raced ahead of the slow pace he had set for her. He suspected she saw right through him when he prolonged the tutoring sessions.

"Meet me tonite when the moon rises," he wrote. "I have something important—" Fearing she could not read the last two words, he scratched out the sentence, the pencil's eraser having long since worn out and substituted "I want to ask you a big favor." He wasn't sure she could read the last word but it was the best he could do.

He folded the note and put it in his pocket as the front wagon pulled away. Slapping the horses lightly with the lines, he pulled into position, jumped to the ground and joined a group of farmers waiting their turn. He knew one or two of the men but most of them were strangers to him.

They had been talking animatedly before he walked up, but hushed as he approached. Surmising that the talk had been of his brother's murder, he decided to put their minds at ease.

"Name's Jed Conover," he said. "I reckon y'all heard about my brother Paul getting killed Tuesday night."

They nodded and one of the men he had seen around town whose name he could not recall said, "Sorry to hear about it," and offered his right hand for Jed to shake. "Will Baker's the name," he said, "I live south of Elk about four miles past your place."

"We've been pretty busy with the funeral and all," Jed said. "We haven't talked to anybody in town. Have you heard if they've made any arrests?"

One of the other men said, "I saw Chuck Timmons yesterday over at Fox and he said they had some good leads but hadn't arrested anybody yet. Word around there is that they're looking for the Sexton boys and one other fellow. Seems like they all skipped the country."

Jed had stationed himself facing his wagon in order to be ready to move when they finished suctioning the cotton. He saw a signal and, saying, "Got to run. Thanks, fellows," he hurried to move his wagon out of the way before he crossed to the post office to buy a stamp and mail his mother's letter to Aunt Betty.

On the way home he left the note in Esther's tree. It was not far from either the road or her house near a stand of blackjacks that the McMasters used as a wood lot. He could see her in the yard dipping buckets of grayish water from the iron pot in which they boiled clothes. She carried the buckets into the house; he knew she would use the water to scrub the floors. Sheets snapped in the freshening wind while shirts and dresses moved as if inhabited. Esther and Beulah ran from the house to remove the starched clothes from the line before the wind blew all the body out of them.

Jed hoped she found time on a busy Saturday to check the tree. He thought she would because he tried to leave a note every Saturday but not knowing for sure kept him on tenterhooks until he left home that evening to meet her.

When he reached their place—a grassy spot among tall elms—moonlight filtering through the leaves lighted the area. She was not there. Thinking she might be hiding behind a tree to tease him, he stepped into the small clearing. Grass brown and dry after three weeks without rain crackled under his feet as he tried to slip up on her. To his sensitive ears, the sound echoed loudly as it bounced from tree to tree.

Leaning against the rough bark of one of the overshadowing elms, he called softly, "Essie, don't play games with me. If you're here, come out. I want to ask you something."

Wind rustled through the trees and fanned his face. He had walked the mile from home, and in his haste to see her, ran most of the way. His damp shirt clung to his back; the breeze felt cool against his skin. Removing his hat, he let the wind play with his thick mane. Esther liked to tousle his hair. Imagining the feel of her fingers tickling his scalp, his desire for her stirred restlessness in him. He paced around the perimeter of the clearing growing more agitated by the minute. Where was she? Had she received his note? He made his way to Esther's tree only to find that the note was gone.

Returning to the grove, he breathed a sigh of relief when he spied her. He stopped to fill his senses with the sight of her. She wore his favorite dress: a dark red creation that looked black in the moonlight and accented her tiny waist. Her dark hair framed her face and cascaded in waves down her back. She had been standing profile to his view when he first saw her but turned at the sound of his footsteps. She took a step toward him and, when he ran to meet her, she ran, too, until they collided and wound their arms tightly around each other. His skin tingled with the feel of her and passion coursed through him.

She giggled.

It was the last sound he wanted to hear. His mission required serious consideration on her part. Unlike their usual meetings of playful teasing and light conversation, tonight's tryst would determine his fate in life. He must talk her into eloping with him and the sooner the better. He rubbed his freshly-shaven cheek against hers and breathed in the light lavender scent she had dabbed behind her ears. Tangling her hair in his hands, he pulled her head back and bent to kiss her.

She jerked her head sideways so that his kiss landed on her cheek. Pulling away from him, she said, "No, Jed, you know we must wait until we're engaged."

Silently he cursed her fastidious adherence to strict courting customs while he seethed with frustration. If she would only kiss him, he was certain he could arouse such a need in her that she would run away with him in an instant. When he felt he could control his voice, he said, "We can be engaged if you'll have me. That's the favor I wanted to ask you. Will you marry me?"

In the moonlight he could see the glow in her eyes and the smile on her lips as she said, "Oh, yes, Jed, yes."

They had been standing an arms-length apart and came together again as if a magnet had drawn them. He held her tightly as he kissed her hair and cheek and then, taking her chin in his hand, he raised her face to his. Again she turned her lips away.

"Damn it, Essie, what's the matter now?"

Stepping away from him, she bit her lip and her eyes glinted in the moonlight with unshed tears.

"I'm sorry," he said. "I know you don't like me to swear in your presence."

"I wish you didn't swear whether you're with me or not," she said. "And I do appreciate it that you didn't take God's name in vain. But I didn't turn my head because I don't want you to kiss me. Oh, I do want that so much. But we aren't really engaged until you ask Pa."

The very thought of asking her father for her hand in marriage filled him with dread. For some reason the man doesn't trust me, he thought. He began again to pace back and forth in the small clearing bypassing Esther who stood in the middle. Somehow he had to convince her to go against her girlhood dreams and become his wife right away without all the fanfare of bridal showers and quilting bees and all that female foolishness.

As he passed by her he saw she was shivering and realized the night wind had turned chilly. He pulled off his jacket and wrapped it around her. It swallowed her. She's so little, he thought, my little sweetheart. He held her until she stopped shivering. She relaxed against him.

He tried a different approach. Turning her in his arms to face him, he said, "Promising to marry me really isn't the biggest favor I wanted to ask. The biggest favor I want you to do for me is to run away with me just like Plez and Flora."

Doubt drew lines between her brows. "But we'd have to lie about our ages."

"That's what Flora did. Are we any better than Flora?" He didn't expect the feeble argument to convince Esther and it didn't.

"I'll be eighteen in January," she said.

Four months, *four* months. A vision of an expanding belly flashed before his eyes. "January!" he exploded. "That's four months. I want you now, Essie, I don't think I can wait that long."

"Oh, Jed, that's so sweet. I don't want to wait, either, really. You can ask my Pa and if both our parents will sign for us, we can get married before then."

He got down on one knee. He heard that worked wonders with women. "Please, Essie, please marry me now. I'll go Monday and get the license. You won't have to tell a lie."

"I can't let you do that. We can't start our married life off with something like that hanging over our heads. If Pa won't sign for me, we'll just have to wait. But, look, we have so much to do getting ready for a wedding. And we'll see each other more often than we do now. Four months will just fly by."

He got up and brushed the dead grass from his pants. She had an answer for every argument he made. He would have to wheedle every time they saw each other. Water dripping on a rock eventually wore it away.

She cocked her head as if listening. "I think I hear our buggy coming. Claude and Horace went to play for a dance tonight and the rest of the family went to town shopping. Arnold and Beulah will be going to school when the cotton is out. Ma wanted to get some material to make dresses and shirts. I had to pretend a headache to get out of going with them. I'd better skedaddle. Hold me one more time."

Jed put his arms around her. He longed to keep her with him always and to hold her any time he wanted. She kissed his temple and said, "I'll talk to Pa and try to smooth the road for you."

He doubted it would do any good. If he couldn't talk her into eloping he didn't stand a chance. When she pushed away to leave, he tried to hold her but she was strong for her size and wriggled out of his arms. He watched her go until she mingled with the shadows and he could no longer see her.

Frustrated, he castigated himself for letting her get the upper hand. He had meant to sweep her off her feet and convince her to run away with him. Maybe I'm so weak because I feel a little bit guilty, he thought. But it means so much to me. If I ever saw a life-and-death situation, this is it.

His father met him at the entrance of the driveway. The fat's in the fire now, he thought, and wondered how to worm his way out of this.

But Matt only said, "I thought I'd take a walk. Things have been getting under my skin this week and I had to get away from the house for a while. It's a pretty night. Walk with me."

Jed wasn't deceived. Pa often took his own good time saying what was on his mind but he'd get around to it sooner or later. And even though he issued the invitation to walk along in the same mild tone, Jed recognized an order when he heard one. He had an all-gone feeling in the pit of his stomach and his legs felt wobbly but he fell into step and walked back along the way he had just traversed.

At the corner, Matt said, "I thought I'd go down to the cemetery. Have you had a chance to see Paul's grave after they decorated it?"

No and I don't want to see it, Jed thought. The idea never crossed my mind. To his father, he said, "I haven't had a minute to think or do anything but work until tonight and I wanted to see Esther."

Uh-oh, mentioning Esther might open the door for his father to bring up the Wade mess. He hurried on, "I had a chance to talk to some men from around the county while I was in town this morning. They think the Sextons have skipped the country."

That distracted Pa. "I wish I could help look for them, but this hits too close to home for me to get involved. I keep thinking I could have found out from Buford where they had the horses stashed, but I thought he could take me there the next day." His voice strangled as he said, "I keep missing my opportunities. I told Paul we'd talk when I got back from the gin that night. We never got the chance. I made Buford tell me what was going on with him and the Sexton boys but I never thought he'd skip out without showing me where they had hid the animals. I went to sleep and let Flora slip off and get married and when I tried to follow them, it was too late."

He fell into a silence Jed was afraid to break. He matched his stride to his father's and counted cadence in his mind. When they reached the cemetery, Matt turned in and Jed cut a square corner to keep step.

Matt led the way to Paul's final resting-place and stood looking down at it in the moonlight. Flowers covering the lumpy mound of red clay softened Jed's shock slightly. He fought back a wave of nausea, turned away from the grave and tried to shut it and all its significance out of his mind. Scenes from his lonely vigil with his brother's body flashed briefly into his mind, disappeared only to be replaced with another. He saw Paul's horse sniffing around the body and seemed to hear its plaintive whinny before he led it away and tethered it. Scampering small animals rattled leaves again in his memory. Shadows of trees lengthened in the moonlight as their leaves soughed in the breeze.

Matt's voice broke into his reverie. "Let's go sit on that bench at the monument."

Jed was so relieved to get away from his memories that he almost welcomed the conversation he had been dreading all day.

Matt didn't mince any words. "What's this I hear about the Wade girl?"

"Pa, why she picked on me at the dance the other night, I don't know. She walked right up to me and asked me to dance with her. I don't know why she was there in the first place. I know she would never have been invited. I only danced with her to keep her from causing a ruckus. Then she whispered to me that she was going to pick a fight with Essie. I got her out of there as fast as I could."

"Umm-hmmm, that much I heard. Why did she want to fight with Esther?"

"I don't know. Sometimes girls like her just like to fight. For some reason, she came after me. I guess she knows Essie and I are sparking."

"I noticed you got to the scene of Paul's ambush somewhat later than the other men. Where did you take her?"

"As far as the road that turns toward their place. I told her to get and not bother me again."

"Jed, I guess I'm going to have to ask you right out. Forgive me if I have misjudged you, Son. Is she pregnant?"

Jed's heart plummeted to the bottom of his stomach. Like Vinnie said about her father finding out, he thought, the fat's in the fire. Aloud, he said, "No."

"You're sure you're telling me the truth? Don't lie to me now."

Jed had stalled until he thought of an answer. "Of course, Pa, I have no way of knowing if she's pregnant. But, if she is, it's not mine."

"Okay, let this be the last I hear of that family. You go on home. I think I'll sit here for a while."

CHAPTER 18

Lillie

During the night the wind freshened and turned to the north. Lillie welcomed the cooler temperature. Lately night sweats had wakened her several times each night; this night was no different. She had lain wide-eyed and still beside her sleeping husband, trying to push back day thoughts and get back to sleep. This time she decided to return to a way that had relaxed her many times in years gone by.

"Lord," she prayed silently. She had never been one to pray aloud but especially now she didn't want to waken Matt. "Dear Father, I come to you repenting of my sins and neglect of my family. I played the role of an invalid when I knew my mind had healed and my spells were a thing of the past. I got used to being coddled and cosseted and I liked it."

A tear slipped from her closed eyelids and she slid from the bed onto her knees. "Forgive me, Father. Help me to be a real mother to the children I have left." Her body shook with sobs she tried to muffle in the bedclothes.

Matt shifted in the bed and groaned as he turned over. This week has been so hard on him, she thought. But he soon settled into a regular breathing pattern again.

She dried her tears and finished her prayer. "Please make me the wife Matt deserves. In Jesus name, Amen."

Crawling back into bed, she pushed her back against Matt's. Without waking, he turned over and put his arm across her. She let herself relax into the curve of his body and soon fell asleep.

Sometime toward morning, the storm began. Rain hit the house with such force that it blew through the open window and across the room to sprinkle their bed. Matt and Lillie jumped up and ran to close other windows throughout the house.

In the kitchen, Matt said, "I'm glad we put the wagon sheet over that little dab of cotton we picked yesterday, but I'd better go see if it's secure enough for this wind."

Lillie closed the door to the girl's bedroom behind her. "I hate for you to go out in this weather," she said.

"No help for it. I'll close the dugout door, too, and wake the boys so they can close the shutters."

"It's so close to morning, I'll make some coffee. When you come back and get dried off, we'll have a quiet time just the two of us." She turned up the collar of his oilskin, stood on tiptoe and kissed him. "It'll be like old times."

He raised one eyebrow as he adjusted his old wide-brimmed felt hat. "I won't be long."

When he returned, Lillie had coffee ready. He stood just inside the back door and slung water from the felt hat sending droplets back into the rain that had settled into a steady downpour. He shut the door, unbuckled his oilskin and, shrugging out of it, hung it on a peg to drip. He took the towel Lillie handed him and wiped his face and smoothed his hair with it.

Lillie poured him a steaming cup of coffee and set it on the table in front of him. "I'll get the cream," she said. She raised a window sash and hastily grabbed a crock from the bay Jed had built on the outside of the window. Screened on three sides with ducking flaps inside the screens and floored with pine planks, the bay window served to keep food cool. Today there was no need to moisten the flaps because the rain had wet them thoroughly.

Lillie removed the clean cloth tied over the crock and skimmed cream into a pitcher. "Things are getting wet in there," she said, "but the butter-dish cover and the lid on the churn will protect them from the weather. I think they'll be all right." She poured a cup of coffee for herself, placed it and the cream pitcher on the table, and sat down.

Matt spooned heavy cream into his coffee, stirred it and took a tentative sip from his mustache cup.

Lillie's musical laugh caused him to return his cup to its saucer and focus his attention on her face.

"Aren't you going to saucer and blow it?" she asked as she raised a spoonful of her own creamed coffee to taste it.

He smiled at her, a smile that didn't quite reach his eyes. She fully understood his somber expression given the events of the last few days. But she worried about him and wanted to lift the heavy burden he carried in some small way. I've let him get in the habit of shielding me, she thought. I have to convince him to let me be a helpmeet, but I don't know how to do it.

She watched him tilt his head back and drain the coffee from his cup. When she refilled his cup, he tipped a good splash of cream into it, stirred vigorously and poured the saucer half full. Raising it to his lips with both hands, he blew noisily. "There," he said, "Satisfied?"

Good, she thought, at least he responded. Laughing, she said, "We're going to be too coffee-logged to get any sleep when we go back to bed."

"I don't think I'll go back to bed," he said. "I'm too tired."

She started to laugh but his expression stopped her. Rimmed by dark circles, his deep-set blue eyes looked glazed as if they saw nothing. Deep grooves outlined the edges of his mustache and extended downward from the corners of his mouth.

"Why don't you sit in the rocking chair and try to rest, then," she said. "The boys can take care of the outside chores."

He set his empty cup on the table and pushed his chair back. "I think I will," he said. "You go on back to bed."

"No, I'll stay up, too." She cast about in her mind for the right words to tell him about her prayers during the night, but she had hidden her deep feelings from him so long that she had forgotten how. Instead, she blurted out, "I'm going to church this morning."

"In this rain?" His back had been turned to her as he sat in the rocker; he scooted the chair sideways and twisted his neck around to look at her.

That got a rise out of him, she thought. "I don't intend to walk," she said. "And the buggy has curtains. Jed will probably be glad to have an excuse to drive it rather than to ride his horse. I'll take Ida and Betsy, too. You go ahead and rest. I'll call you when breakfast is ready."

At breakfast that morning when Lillie announced her intention of attending church, Matt said, "I wish you'd change your mind. It's a bad day to get out."

I wonder if he knows how much I'm tempted to back out, she thought. But if I don't go today, I may not have the courage by next Sunday. She said, "Jed, were you going to try to go?"

"Yes, Ma. I thought I'd borrow Pa's slicker and ride my horse. But if you want to go, we can take the buggy."

Ida and Betsy sounded like harmony when they said, "I want to go."

"That settles it, then," Lillie said. "We'll get ready and go."

"Ma, we need to set out early," Jed said. "That road may be pretty slick."

The road turned out to be slicker than they expected. Twice in the first mile the rig slid sideways on the slippery red clay roadbed and Jed had to get out and lead the horse until the buggy pulled straight behind. He kept to the middle of the road; no other conveyance had passed that way and they did not meet anyone. When they reached the McMasters' farmstead, they found ruts made by their wagon as it turned into the road. Once Jed managed to maneuver the buggy wheels into one of the wagon ruts they proceeded apace and soon covered the last two miles to the meetinghouse.

Only two vehicles other than the McMasters' farm wagon stood in the churchyard. "Looks like a short turnout this morning," Jed said as he steered the rig under the roof extension on the front of the building. Lillie and the girls alighted from the buggy as dry and comfortable as if they had not traversed over three miles of sticky red clay. They waited while Jed parked the rig and joined them.

Jed had not fared as well—mud spatters covered his clothing—but he cleaned the soles and heel of his boots on the mud-scraper mounted on the edge of the top step. Doffing his hat and slicker he shook them vigorously before he went inside and hung them on pegs on the back wall. He slicked his wet hair with his hands and wiped his hands on his shirt.

Lillie decided he compared favorably with the other men. She recognized all of those assembled. Joe Dave Goodgion and his brother, Leon, sat on the front seat along with Everett McMasters. Four little girls sat side by side on the second row: Beulah McMasters and Prudence Goodgion's granddaughters. Betsy pulled away from her mother's hand and ran to sit by them. Jed joined the three McMasters boys on the back seat directly behind Esther. Ida scooted in on the other side of Polly Wilson. Several empty benches separated the young people from the pew where Prudence sat with her daughters-in-law and Judith McMasters. Judith moved over on the bench, patted the place, and nodded to invite Lillie to sit with her.

Shortly after Lillie took the offered seat, Everett pulled his pocket watch from his vest pocket and consulted it. Standing, he faced the congregation. "It's ten minutes past starting time," he said. "We tarried for one another as the good book says and, sure enough, our number swelled. But now we'll wait no longer. Let's start with an old song everybody knows: *I Am Thine, O Lord.*" Starting with the topmost note in the soprano, he sang down the scale and back to the first note, "Do, sol, me, do, sol, do, mi." Positioning his right hand to beat the time, he said, "On the downbeat," and began to lead the song.

Lillie knew the words well but had no ear for music. She sang softly but it didn't matter; Judith's strong alto covered any mistake she made. On the chorus she forgot her timidity as the words expressed the prayer in her heart:

> "Draw me nearer, nearer, blessed Lord,
> "To the cross where Thou hast died;
> "Draw me nearer, nearer, nearer, blessed Lord,
> "To thy precious, bleeding side."

Everett held up his hand palm outward at the end of the chorus. "Everybody sing right out now. Make a joyful noise unto the Lord. On the second."

They finished the song and sang two more before Joe David Goodgion rose to preach. As he read the scripture and called on his brother Leon to lead prayer, Lillie found it hard to keep her mind from wandering. She prayed her own heartfelt prayer for courage. During the night she had wakened several times and rehearsed in her mind the steps she planned to take to turn her life around. Foremost had been her decision to return to church. The sudden onslaught of rain and subsequent steady downpour had seemed both a blessing and a stumbling block. Even after they started out, when the buggy skidded toward the ditch, she feared they would have to turn back home.

But they made it here and she had breathed a sigh of relief. She had enjoyed the songs especially listening to the fine voices of the talented McMasters family. Now, as the worship service progressed, she felt apprehension increase by the minute. *I'll wait until the last verse* of the invitation song to go forward, she thought. That decided, she focused her attention on the preacher and found he was drawing the sermon to a close. She saw Everett stand and announce the hymn: *Lord, I'm Coming Home.*

"Let's stand and sing this song slowly and with expression," he said.

Lillie did not know the song. She listened carefully as the rest of the congregation sang and wondered how she would recognize the last verse. The words of the second stanza echoed in the room:

> "I've wasted many precious years,
> "Now I'm coming home;
> "I now repent with bitter tears,
> "Lord, I'm coming home."

Bitter tears spilled down Lillie's cheeks as she stepped into the aisle and stumbled forward. Joe Dave took her hand and led her to a seat on the front bench. She hid her face in her handkerchief as the song continued. She felt a slight vibration of the bench as more people joined her but she didn't look up.

Joe Dave sat beside her and touched her shoulder. "What is your desire, Lillie?" he asked.

She opened her eyes then and saw Jed, Ida, and Polly sitting beside her. Shaken, she fixed her gaze on the man waiting for her reply. "I have many things to be made right," she said. "They are of a personal nature and I ask for your prayers for strength and courage. I want forgiveness for neglecting the assembly and want to be a part of this fellowship."

Joe Dave straightened and addressed the assembly. "Our brother and our sisters have come forward this morning asking for your prayers. Ida and Polly state that they have deceived their parents and that it is widely known. Jed wants to rededicate his life. Lillie confesses that she has been out of duty and wants to join herself to this flock. Join me, please, while I pray."

Lillie felt great relief as the prayer ended and she rose to return to her seat for the rest of the worship. For the first time since she had left Texas, she partook of the Lord's Supper. After the last song and final prayer, the women surrounded her, hugging her and wiping tears of their own. All the men shook her hand and uttered words of welcome.

When she descended the steps, she felt cool air against her face. The rain had stopped and the trees surrounding the churchyard cast short shadows in the bright noon sunshine. Peace filled her being as she settled in the buggy with Betsy on her lap to begin the ride home.

CHAPTER 19

Ben

Ben overslept Monday morning. Cooler air as a result of Sunday's rain had crept into the dugout bringing with it a need for more cover. They hadn't kept extra quilts down there over the hot summer. Sometime during the night, Holt had crawled into bed with him and Jed. Three in the double bed made sleeping impossible for Ben. He hunted through the dirty clothes tub until he found two shirts and a pair of pants, put them on, and wrapped up in the sheet on the other bed.

A shaft of bright sunshine filtering through the shutters hit his eyes and brought him instantly to his feet. He checked the other bed. Empty. Without bothering to change clothes, he padded barefoot across the yard to the kitchen door carrying his shoes and socks. He set his shoes on the step they had made from a large flat rock and splashed his face and neck with cold water from the wash pan. Shivering, he rubbed vigorously with the clean ducking towel hanging from a nail on the wall.

Closing the five-panel door behind him, he leaned against it a moment and let the warmth of the room sink to his bones. Holt, the only other occupant of the room, sat with elbows on knees, hunched over a tin bucket on the floor. He had not stopped whittling when

Ben entered the room and answered Ben's cheery "Good morning" with a grunt.

"Good morning, Benjamin, and how are you today?" Ben said.

Holt looked up from his work and grinned. "Sorry," he said. "I want to work on this while everybody is gone."

Ben dragged a chair close to the kitchen range, sat and pulled on both socks while his shoes warmed. Holt seemed so absorbed in his whittling that Ben circled the table and went to his side to look at it. He could feel shavings through his heavy work socks the last step or two.

"You'd better clean up these shavings before Ma gets back," he said. "What're you making?"

Holt held up a flat piece of pine six inches long and about the breadth of two fingers. He had reduced one end to half-thickness for the last half-inch and had started to make the other end match it.

"Paul had started this doll bed for Betsy's birthday. This is the last upright for the headboard. Jed said he'd help me figure the size I need for the footboard." He went back to his work. "I still have a lot to do so I need to keep at it."

Ben thought, I've been gone longer than I realized. Holt had grown not only in size but manner and abilities. "Is that the knife I gave you for Christmas?" he asked. "Let me see if you've learned how to keep it sharp."

Holt folded the knife and handed it to him. Ben opened it and, feeling along the blade gingerly with his thumb, found it razor-sharp. He folded it and handed it back.

"I guess that'll pass," he said. "Where is everybody?"

"Pa saddled Spot right after breakfast and rode off. Said he was going to find Deputy Timmons and see how the investigation is going before he comes home. He was crying when he climbed aboard Paul's horse, but he said the horse needed the work-out." The boy's voice choked on the last word and he fell silent.

Ben wrapped the lace around the second boot-top and tied it in front. The mention of his father's grief struck him in the pit of his stomach and he sat for a minute before checking the warming oven for breakfast. He carried a plate of biscuits and a bowl of gravy to the table and set them down. Stealing a covert glance at Holt, he saw the youngster wipe his eyes on his sleeve.

Turning his back to Holt, he said, "And?"

By the time Holt answered, Ben had transferred plate and silverware to the table and filled a cup with warmed-over coffee. He took a sip, grimaced and added more cream.

"Ma heard at church yesterday that two stores in Wilson are having a big sale. She made Jed drive her and Betsy down there and, of course, Ida had to go along. They took a lunch and will be gone all day. I should get a lot done on this bed before they get back. What are you going to do today?"

"It's still too wet to get in the cotton patch and besides, with all the help we had last week, we'll have to wait for more bolls to open. I think the first thing I'll do is take a hoe and rake and go work on smoothing up Paul's grave. Maybe I can break up the clods after this rain. After that, I think I'll come back and get my gun and go squirrel hunting. They're beginning to eat pecans now and a mess of them should be mighty tasty."

Hoe and rake across his left shoulder, Ben turned the corner south toward Pendleton Cemetery. It felt good to stretch his legs and breathe the fresh fall air. He shifted the tools to his right shoulder, shaded his eyes with his left hand, and gauged the distance the sun had traveled from the horizon. Judging it to be at least three hours high, he whistled. He bet he could count on the fingers of one hand the number of times he had slept that late since he was ten years old. The family must have left nearly two hours before.

The whistle had changed to a cheery tune by the time he reached the cemetery, but once there the tune died on his lips. Spot grazed untethered near Paul's grave and, standing with his back to the road,

Matt presented a desolate figure beside the red-clay-covered mound. Had he already been to Fox, found Timmons and returned? No, he hadn't had time. Maybe he had run into him in Chagris. No, the horse had been unsaddled. With a sinking feeling, Ben knew the pair had come here directly from home.

His father hadn't heard him walk up. Spot raised his head, turned and looked at Ben then returned to his forage. What should he do? Slip away and never let Pa know he saw him? No, he couldn't leave Pa alone. Despondency manifested itself in the set of his sagging shoulders, the angle of his bowed head, and the limpness of his arms hanging at his side. Ordinarily Pa would have heard him whistling. He wasn't that far away. It could be that he was losing his hearing; he was an old man.

Ben yelled, "Pa, is that you?"

Matt turned slowly as if he were pushing against a great force. When he saw Ben striding toward him, he said, "Oh. Son. What are you doing here?"

Ben thought, I could ask you the same question. But he said, "I thought I'd try to smooth up Paul's grave after this rain. It was a pile of red clay clods. When I get that done, I'm going squirrel hunting."

Matt shifted his gaze to the tools as Ben laid them on the ground. "Good idea," he said. His voice sounded lifeless. But he removed the key to the ammunition box from his bib pocket and handed it to Ben.

That worried Ben. Pa had always been energetic and wanted to run everything. In their little world, his word had always been law. Ben stooped to retrieve the hoe and chopped at a clod. He looked at his father out of the corner of his eye. Any other time, Matt would have offered suggestions or else started raking. He broke up a few more clods. Still his father stood silently beside him.

"I'm a little thirsty after that walk over here," Ben said. "Do they have any water around here?"

Matt shook his body as one trying to wake from a bad dream. "Yes, there's a well over by the monument. You can draw a bucket of water. I could use a drink myself." He led the way and Ben followed.

Ben drew the water and offered the bucket to his father. Matt took a long gulp and handed it back to him. Ben put the edge of the bucket to his lips and felt cool water fill his mouth and slide down his dry throat. He spilled a little onto his shirtfront and relished the wetness. The early morning breeze had died and the sun's rays pulling moisture from the earth portended a hot, humid day.

"Let's go sit on that bench in the shade," he said. He closed the well's cover and set the bucket of water on the lid.

They sat side by side on the bench. Fearful of looking directly at his father, Ben fixed his attention on the display of autumn flowers. He fanned with his hat and tried to compose the questions he planned to ask. Go roundabout and ease up on them, he decided.

"Pa, thank you for letting me sleep awhile this morning," he said. "I needed it after this last week."

Matt didn't reply.

Ben tried expanding on the same theme. "I left Texas a week ago Sunday," he said. "Let me tell you it wasn't an easy trip in that rough wagon. I got here Tuesday tired and wanting nothing more than a good meal and a soft bed. So what happens? We hurry up and go to a play party. And before it's over, things took a turn for the worse."

He paused and stole a sideways glance at Matt. Pa's blue eyes (had they faded in the past few days?) stared into the distance from under his craggy forehead and thick eyebrows. His mustache began to tremble and his chin to quiver.

Ben switched his attention to the stone monolith in the center of the garden and continued his recitation. "Paul was ambushed and they haven't found the dastardly villains yet. None of us got any sleep that night. Then came the day of preparation. I was so tired by then that I didn't know when my head hit the pillow that night. The rest of the week is a blur." A glimpse of Matt's profile showed him that Pa had mastered his emotions. Ben turned to face him. "Pa, have you been getting any rest?"

The direct question broke Matt's concentration. He shifted his scrutiny to the monolith. "Not very much, no," he said. "Ben, I keep running things over and over in my mind. I think, what could I have done differently? Where did I go wrong? I kept missing my opportunities. I told Paul we'd talk when I got back from the gin that night. We never got the chance." His eyes brimmed with tears and he fished for a handkerchief in his hip pocket, wiped them away, and blew his nose noisily. "I made Buford tell me what was going on with him and the Sexton boys but I never thought he'd skip out without showing me where they had hid the animals." He set his square jaw and stared once more into the distance. "Then I misjudged Flora. It never occurred to me that she would disobey me. I went to sleep and let her slip off and get married and when I tried to follow them, it was too late."

As Ben listened to Matt's recitation, he tried to figure out which one—Buford or Flora—incited his Pa's anger the most. One thing he knew for sure; he'd try his best to keep on his father's good side. To bring out that good side must be his goal. He said, "Pa, you can't blame yourself for anything that's happened."

Matt cut him off. "I do blame myself, Ben. I blame myself for it all. If I hadn't been so blamed anxious to deliver the first load of cotton to the gin…Plague take it, Ben, the extra money can never compensate for my boy's life. As it turned out, I'd heard wrong and they were only paying a half of a cent more. And since they based that price on quality, it was mine at any time. If I had just listened to Paul…He asked me what to do about turning Buford over to the authorities. I put him off. If I hadn't, he might not have stumbled on their hideout. I'm certain as I live and breathe today that one of the Sexton boys saw him and killed him for what he knew."

Change the subject. "Pa, have you been coming here to the graveyard often?"

"Every day, Ben, every day."

"What do you do down here?" Ben looked around. Except for the evidence of Sunday morning's rain, he saw no change from the day of the funeral.

Matt favored Ben with a look of pity. "It's only natural, Son. I stand at the grave and talk to Paul."

It doesn't seem natural to me, Ben thought, Paul's not here. "You come here by yourself every day and talk to Paul?"

"No, I brought Jed with me Saturday night. And I don't spend all my time talking to Paul. I sit here part of the time and remember. Besides, I'm not the only one. After your Ma delivered dishes Friday, I found buggy tracks in the dead grass."

Change the subject again. "Pa, what do you think is going to happen to Buford?"

"That subject is closed as far as I'm concerned. I don't want to talk about either him or Flora. Don't you understand, Ben? I'm a failure as a father, a complete failure. I don't want to be reminded."

I hope he doesn't include me, Ben thought. "Pa, I don't think you're a failure; you've got more kids than them."

"Some of them aren't grown, either. Now, you, Ben, you've turned out fine so far. You're the one I know I can depend on. But Jed—Jed's in some kind of trouble. He's hiding something; I think he's lying to me. I tried to pin him down Saturday night, but he evaded every direct question I put to him."

He put both hands on his thighs and pushed himself up from the bench. Biting his lip and letting out a deep breath, he put his hand to the small of his back and rubbed. "I've got a little rheumatism," he said. "Catch my horse and saddle him for me, will you, Ben. I need to get around if I'm going to find Timmons today."

Worry pulled Ben's brows down toward his nose and tears filled his eyes as he watched his father ride off. He drew his thumb and middle finger across them and pinched his nose, sniffing back the tears. The crisp fall air and warm sunshine seemed a mockery; he would finish the task that brought him here and leave. Trudging to the grave, he picked up the hoe and attacked clods with a vengeance.

Working on the grave until it passed his inspection occupied the next two hours. Mr. Pendleton had shuffled over and complimented him on a job well done. He felt a sense of accomplishment as he always did when he jumped right in, worked on a distasteful task and laid it by. There, now, he thought as he surveyed the smooth mound, that's over and done with.

He took long steps on the walk home to stretch his leg and back muscles. By the time he turned the corner near the McIntosh place, he had begun to whistle a march and to match his stride to the tune.

Holt stood at the dining table fitting the headboard of the doll bed together. Ben stopped beside him and watched him work for a minute before he set about preparing their meal. He saw the way the uprights fit in grooves in the crosspieces and shook his head.

"That's clever," he said. "Those uprights can slide together and make a solid unit or be pushed apart for a different look. I can just see Betsy playing with it. How did you put in the grooves?"

"I don't know; Paul did it. Jed knows how, but I'll have to wait until he comes home to show me." He wiggled the crosspieces into grooves in the end uprights. "I wish I knew how to do it. I have all afternoon with nothing to do."

Ben built a little fire in the cook stove, poured out the stale coffee and sloshed water into the pot. Without measuring he dumped in ground coffee and set it to boil. He carried biscuits and fried side meat from the warming oven to the table. "Make yourself useful," he told Holt. "Peel us an onion and we'll make sandwiches."

While he filled their cups with coffee he sent Holt to get cream from the bay window. After returning thanks, they made their sandwiches and creamed their coffee. Ben studied the concentration on Holt's face. He thought, he's enjoying this, just us two men.

Holt tasted his coffee and made a face. "That's the strongest coffee I ever put in my mouth," he said.

Ben laughed. "Put more cream in it, and quit fussing."

I'm enjoying this, too, he thought. I wish I could take him hunting with me this afternoon, but he's too young. We'll have to figure out something for him to do. I wish I had the knack for making things that he and Jed and Paul have. With a stab of remembrance he changed the thought to "Paul had."

"I tell you what let's do, Holt," he said. "Let's measure how tall a footboard is compared to a headboard and you can start whittling the uprights for it."

Holt glowed. "That'll work," he said. "But we don't need to measure. I can just eyeball it and figure it out."

I'll bet he can, Ben thought. I'd have to measure and figure and measure again. Aloud, he said, "How old are you now?"

"I'll be twelve in November. I get to go back to school this year. I was so happy last year when we moved up here and they didn't have a school for me to go to. But I didn't like it as much as I thought I would. I'm ready to start as soon as the cotton is picked."

Ben, whose schooling had ended after third grade, agreed. "Get all the schooling you can. It's okay for me to quit because I never did want to be anything but a farmer. And I learned to cipher. That's easy for me; I can do it in my head. But with the talent you have, you can be anything you want."

Having eaten all the food in sight, they pushed back their chairs and left the dirty dishes and empty coffeepot on the table. Holt went to the woodshed to hunt a piece suitable for making slats and Ben got his Stevens .22 single-shot from the corner behind the quilt curtain. When he searched the ammunition box, he found only six bullets to fit his gun and made a mental note to buy more when he went to town.

Stump McIntosh had given permission to hunt anywhere on his land, but Ben felt he should let him know his intentions. As he cut through the woods toward McIntosh's house, he kept an eagle eye out for game. He didn't expect to find any in that location so told his landlord that he would like to hunt in his pecan bottom. Once there, he selected a fallen log and settled on it to still-hunt.

In the interval it took for the squirrels to reappear, he surveyed his surroundings. Large pecan trees dotted the landscape but failed to crowd out saplings and underbrush. Splintered dead limbs pointing toward the ground from the tops of every tree recalled the devastating ice storm from three or four years past. This grove needs work, he thought remembering the clean orchards in his native Texas. He could do a lot with this place; his hands itched to be at work on it.

Hearing a scolding chatter, he turned his attention to the trees in his immediate vicinity. Two squirrels appeared to be laying claim to the same limb. Ben carefully lifted the gun from across his lap and quietly raised it to his shoulder. When he had a squirrel's head in his sights, he squeezed the trigger. The shot sounded deafening in his ears and the other squirrel disappeared before the dead one hit the ground.

Ben reloaded and laid the twenty-two back across his lap. He sat without moving until another squirrel ventured into sight. After killing one more squirrel, he retrieved both of them and walked to another stand. Still-hunting is so different from hunting with a dog, he thought. But it serves me right for trying to steal Uncle Prent's dog. I think I'll ask Pa if it's all right to get a dog and then I'll start looking for me one.

Ben hunted until he exhausted his ammunition. When he returned home with the six squirrels, he saw Spot drinking at the water trough. Holt sat on a stump whittling. Leaving the squirrels hanging outside, he washed up and went in the house to hunt his father.

Matt sat stretched out in the big wing chair, his stocking feet resting on the footstool in front of him. Ben pulled a dining chair close to the wing chair, turned it backward and straddled it.

"Did you have any luck finding Timmons?" he asked.

Matt rubbed his hand over his face from his forehead to his chin as if clearing his mind. "Yes, I went all the way to Fox and they told me he was in Chagris. I guess I should have gone there first. Anyway, he told me they found the horses. It seems that the Sextons had abandoned them, left them to starve in the corral they had fashioned. I had told them that Buford indicated that the corral was about five miles from our place. So they drew a circle on the map and scouted around that area. Some of the owners of the stolen horses helped the deputies and formed a posse. One of them found the horses Sunday afternoon. They were hungry and, if it hadn't been for the rain, they would have had no water after they drank the tub dry."

"So what did they do with the horses?"

"Took them to the wagon yard in Chagris. They're going to let the owners pick them up and take them home if they can establish ownership."

"What about the Sexton boys?"

"No sign of them so far. But they'll get them. Someone knows more than they're telling and they will come forward eventually. They always do." Matt sighed and pushed the footstool away. Putting his feet on the floor, he reached for his boots. "Did you get any squirrels?"

"Half a dozen. I need to get the whet rock and sharpen my knife so I can clean them."

"I'll help you. Your Ma will be surprised when she sees what she has to cook for supper."

CHAPTER 20

Jed

Thinking back over the past week's events produced such pain that Jed shoved the memories to the back of his mind and tried to concentrate on plans. He felt he had laid the groundwork for advancing his courtship campaign. After church yesterday he had managed a few minutes alone with Esther. She had been so thrilled over his confession that he thought she would embrace him right there in front of the whole congregation. He should have known her better than that. But she did hold his hand as he drew her aside.

"Did you get a chance to talk to your Pa?" he asked.

"Not yet, but I'll make a point to do it today. Surely he'll be impressed with your rededication this morning. I'm so happy. I don't know how to tell you how happy I really am."

That's what I was hoping when I went forward, he thought. Strike while the iron is hot. "Then will you tell him I want to come over and have a talk with him tomorrow night? Do you think that will be all right?"

She had agreed, and now as he guided the horse and buggy down the road toward Wilson, he felt good about his prospects.

"Ma, could I have some money to buy Essie a present?" he asked. "I thought if you help me I might find some dress goods she will like and get a length for her to make a new dress."

Ida snorted. "Jed, you are hopeless. Don't you know you don't buy clothes for a woman that's not your wife?"

"That's right, Jed," Lillie said. "It puts her in a bad light and can ruin her reputation. But I'm sure your Pa gave me enough money that we can find something for a gift for Essie. A brooch might be nice, or some ribbons for her hair. We'll see what the stores have in stock."

Altogether the day had turned out well. They found a cameo that could be worn either as a breastpin or on a ribbon as a necklace. Adding a piece of black velvet ribbon had only cost three cents and, as Ida said, just made the gift extra special. Comments like that from his moon-eyed sister meant more to him than he intended to let her know. Probably all girls liked romantic presents. Esther lived in a dream world as far as he could tell. She had high ideals and thought he was a knight in shining armor like those old-timey tales. Let her think that way until they were married; it made his suit easier. She'd come down to earth soon enough after the wedding.

He paid particular attention to each detail that evening as he prepared to present his case to Esther's father. He stropped his razor to a fine edge, worked up a heavy lather in the shaving cup, and steamed his face with a towel wrung out in a pan of hot water. When he finished scraping off the second soaping, he felt every inch of his face and neck with the tips of his fingers and pronounced the effort a job well done. After taking a thorough sponge bath, he donned clean clothing and brushed his dress boots to a high shine. Patting pomade on his hair, he parted it in the middle and combed it as smooth and flat as the natural curl would let him. It was a little long in the back but in all the hullabaloo of the past week he hadn't had time for Ma to trim it. It would have to do.

When he alighted from his horse at the McMasters' place, he patted the breast pocket of his suit coat to make sure he had remembered to bring the little package containing the brooch and ribbon. It hadn't moved since he had last checked it on the way over there. Arnold ran out to meet him and he let the excited fourteen-year-old take care of his horse. Was all the family aware of his mission?

He was sure that was the case when Mr. McMasters answered his knock. The rest of the family had apparently busied themselves elsewhere. Even Arnold did not reappear. However, Mr. McMasters seemed cordial enough, shaking his hand as he led him in and offered him a chair. McMasters took a chair facing Jed and proceeded to take his time filling his pipe, tamping the tobacco to his satisfaction, and puffing until the lighted match almost burned his fingers. He blew out smoke, took the pipe from his mouth and sat waiting without having said a word.

Jed felt at a distinct disadvantage and knew McMasters had planned it that way. All his rehearsals fled from his consciousness and he wanted to jump up from that chair and run away as fast as his legs would carry him. But every day, nay every hour that ticked by spelled doom for him. Gripping the curved ends of the chair's wooden arms, he cleared his throat.

"Mr. McMasters, I reckon you know why I am here." He hadn't looked at Esther's father. I have to look him in the eye, he thought. It won't do any good to plead my case otherwise. He made a valiant effort and succeeded in holding the man's attention with his gaze. "I have come to ask for your daughter's hand in marriage." I sound like a dime novel, he thought.

McMasters clamped the pipe between his teeth, inhaled and exhaled several times, and withdrew the pipe. "Esther advised me of your intentions," he said. A fleeting smile flickered on his lips. "I have considered the matter. It appears to me that the two of you are in agreement and that my opinion is irrelevant."

He stuck the pipe back in his mouth, scratched a match on the instep of his shoe, and sucked until the tobacco lighted again. Jed breathed a sigh of relief. The old man was going to listen to reason. He waited politely.

McMasters said, "But I'm going to voice my opinion, anyway. I believe both of you are too young to get married. Esther has all the skills to be a good housewife, but she hasn't grown up emotionally. She has her head in the clouds. I see you as an impulsive young man without the maturity to be the head of your own household or to lead a family as a man should. For those reasons, I have decided to withhold my permission. Esther will be eighteen in January and then she can do as she pleases."

Jed's heart sank, but he had to make one more try. "Mr. McMasters," he began.

But the older man held up his hand to stop him. "My mind is made up," he said. "However, I won't deny you her company and you may announce your betrothal and prepare for the wedding." He rose and looked down at Jed. "And now, I expect you will want to talk to Esther. I'll go call her and leave the two of you alone."

Esther must have been waiting at the door because as soon as her father left the room she ran in. Her face expressed complete happiness—her eyes sparkled, her wide grin exposed her dimples and even, white teeth. She hurried to him, arms outstretched.

He wrapped her in his arms and this time, when he bent to kiss her on the mouth, she didn't turn away. It was a sweet kiss but not the passionate response he had anticipated. She was like a flower still in the bud; he would have the task of helping her bloom. It would have been a joy to watch her blossom, to bring her gently from girl to woman, if he had time. If only he had time.

Esther said, "Oh, Jed, isn't it wonderful? Now we can see each other when we choose. And we can make plans for our wedding and our home. I have lots of things in my hope chest. I can't wait to show them to you." She snuggled against him.

He kissed her again, tried to make it a long kiss but she pulled away. "Come, let's sit on the duofold and talk." She led him to the leather couch that could be opened to make a bed.

Jed sat beside her and tried to think how to cajole her away from her dreams and to convince her to elope. He held her hands and slid to his knees in front of her. "Essie, I don't want to wait. I want our dreams fulfilled now. I want to make you my wife without going through all this folderol of big weddings and shivarees and all that. Let's make plans and slip off without telling anybody."

Her expression wavered between doubt and desire. Cinch the desire if you can. The gift, give her the gift. He reached in his pocket and removed the small tissue-wrapped package. Laying it in her hand, he said, "I wish it was a ring."

She laid the gift in her lap and slowly undid it. He could tell she savored every tiny movement that uncovered the hidden articles. She was like a child at Christmas and he realized that she had received few unexpected presents in her life. Lifting the narrow black velvet ribbon, she let the length of it trail over her fingers as she bent forward to kiss him on the forehead. "Oh, Jed, it's so pretty. And there is so much I can do with it. Thank you."

He didn't know what to say. Had she not seen the cameo? Apparently not, because she started to replace the ribbon in the tissue. Watching her face when she spied the pin made his heart jump with a thrill he would remember all his life. She sucked in her breath, her lips forming a small, round "o" of pleasure. Her eyes widened as she picked it up and sat very still looking at it.

He could stand it no longer. Rising from his knees, he pulled her to her feet, crushing her to him, kissing her soft lips. This time she kissed him in a different way, but he considered it more gratitude than passion. Still holding her tightly, he put his lips close to her ear and whispered, "Come away with me, my little love, come away with me tonight."

Esther pulled away from him, took a step backward, fell onto the duofold. The cameo and ribbon spilled to the floor, the tissue paper fluttering after them. She leaned over just as he stooped to pick them up and they banged their heads together with a sharp crack. Holding his head, he raised up to look at her. She looked dazed as she clamped her hand to her forehead.

"Esther?" His voice squeaked as he uttered the one-word question through his tight throat.

Her eyes focused when she heard the concern in his voice and she looked directly at him. She stared a moment rubbing her head and then burst into a fit of laughter. "You should see us," she said. "We look exactly alike, both holding our heads in our hands. What a way to end such a wonderful evening."

He tried to laugh with her but found it too difficult. He felt he was losing any advantage the gift had given him. "Sweetheart, I don't want this evening ever to end. I want to take you with me and be together always."

Her expression sobered. She took his hand and pulled him down to sit beside her. "Jed, you're so sweet. I thought you were just being romantic, but you mean it, don't you? Oh, my dearest, don't you see that we can't run away? I will not, cannot, disobey my father. Nor can I lie about my age." She put a finger to his lips as he started to protest. "And I won't let you lie for me. There's nothing for it but to wait until January. And I promise you that I'll make the time so pleasurable that it will pass in a flash."

Disappointment made him speechless. He retrieved the cameo and ribbon and placed them in her hand, closed the fingers over them. Then he stood and looked around for his hat.

She rose, too, laid the gifts on a table, and put her hand on his arm. "Oh, Jed, I know you're disappointed, but don't look like it's the end of the world. Our life, our world, is just beginning. It really won't be long before we can be together all the time. I want to be your wife more than you can know. But it has to be right for everybody concerned. We aren't the only ones involved; there's your family and my family. And we want our friends to be part of it. Come on, Jed, say it's all right."

"It's all right for now, but I won't give up. I want you so much. So be prepared." He held her one more time but didn't try to kiss her again.

On the ride home, he talked to his horse. "We'll see who wins this one, Blaze. She's stubborn but it's a matter of life and death to me. We'll see who wins."

CHAPTER 21

Lillie

On Sunday three weeks later, Polly Wilson told Lillie that her father, the postmaster, sent word that she had a letter waiting at the post office. The next time one of the men took a load of cotton to the gin, he called for the mail and brought the letter home.

Lillie took it to her room and opened it with her scissors. Dragging her little sewing rocker near the window, she smoothed the pages open and read the flowing script. Betty's penmanship almost overflowed the constricting lines of the ruled paper.

October 16, 1907

My dear sister Lillie,

I will try to write a few lines to express my sorrow and that of all our family for your recent tragedy. How my heart aches for you, my dearest sister. I pray God will ease your heartache as only He can. I know it will take time.

I must tell you that your family here in Texas held our own memorial for our dear Paul. I wrote our brother, Benjamin, and when he and his family came down, our sisters Cordelia and Isabelle came to our house with all their families. Prentiss gave a talk—reading Scripture and telling a little bit about Paul's life. Delia's girls sang two songs.

(They have the sweetest voices. They must have gotten them from their Pa's side as none of us could ever carry a tune.) Then Bennie said a prayer.

I always had a special place in my heart for Paul. When you were so sick and I helped take care of your two little boys, I fell in love with both of them. But Paul was nothing more than a baby himself and I felt from that time on that he was one of my own.

I hope things work out okay for Flora and her man. She is so young but you were two years younger when you married the first time. Well, enough of that! Some of her girl friends at church and their mothers had a shower for her when I told them she got married. I have boxed up all the gifts and am sending them to her at General Delivery, Chagris. You didn't tell me the name of her husband so I will just address it to Flora Conover. If the Postmaster doesn't know her, you might tell him where to find her.

I hope my memories haven't added to your grief. I wish you could just get on the train and come to my house for a month or two but I understand that your family needs you right now. Maybe Delia, Belle, and I can get on the train ourselves and come up there when the crops are all in. We'll try to do that, sweet sister.

I must close for now. Write again soon. Give my love to all your family.

Your sister, Betty

P. S. A funny thing happened about the time that I got your letter. Our old squirrel dog, Bob, went missing. He was gone about a week, but we got up one morning and found him tied to a spoke of the wagon wheel. I'll always wonder where he was and who tied him up when they brought him home. B. W.

CHAPTER 22

Esther

"Ma, do you know where I can find the cords to swing the quilt frames from the ceiling?" Esther called as she pulled out one drawer after another in the sewing machine cabinet. "Flora will be here any minute."

Her mother replied without leaving her bedroom. "They're in here. Remember, we wrapped the frames with those cords and stashed them under our bed. You need to concentrate on finding the big needles and twine to sew the quilt in the frames. They should be in the machine drawer."

"No, I've already looked there. I'll keep looking." Frustrated, she mumbled, "I just wish we could have a place for everything instead spending half our time hunting for something."

She expected Flora to step on the porch any minute. Now that she had married Plez Wilson she lived across the road. The newlyweds had moved in with his father while Plez built a house for them on his own acreage. Each enrolled Indian had received one hundred sixty acres as an allotment. Plez had chosen his land in the same section as Mr. Wilson but north of him. When they get their own home, Esther thought, she'll be just a half-mile away. She envisioned herself as Jed's wife and the two sisters-in-law raising their children in the new state about to be solemnized by the marriage of Oklahoma Territory and Indian Territory.

The two girls had spent hours in the past few days carding cotton to be used as batting. Esther's twelve-year-old sister, Beulah, had pestered them to teach her to use the cards but she could not get the hang of reversing the paddles to pull the finished product from the fine teeth through which they combed the cotton into smooth batts. Finally, Esther became exasperated. "We'll never get these done in time if you keep slowing us down. Just leave us alone."

Beulah jumped down from the pile of cotton on which she sat and stomped away, flinging a threat over her shoulder. "I'll get you, Miss Smarty."

"You two remind me of Ida and me," Flora said. "Why is it sisters can't get along?"

"I think you and Ida will be friends some day. You're as different as black and white, but Ida will grow up some day. I don't know about Beulah, though. She is slow about most things. You saw how she was all thumbs when she tried to use the cards. It's the same way with everything but music. She started playing the organ when she was three years old. We didn't have a piano, but Mrs. Wilson let her practice on theirs and she picked it right up. But nothing else came easily to her. She can read pretty well. Sister Goodgion took pity on her because the schools weren't open to any but Indians. She taught her to read and write. I wish the Goodgions had lived here when I was little."

"Yes, they've been a blessing to this community. No longer than we've lived here I can see that. But I thought Jed has been teaching you."

"He was, but now that we're engaged he keeps pestering me to run off and marry him. We're beginning to argue all the time. And I wish I could talk to him about that incident with Vinnie. I think about it a lot but I'm hesitant to bring it up because I'm afraid, if I do, I'll lose him."

"A team of wild horses couldn't drag Jed away from you, Essie. I know my brother and he loves you with all his heart." She deftly turned the carding boards and lifted a batt of cotton that she placed on a stack. "I can't tell you how much I appreciate your giving me the cotton for my quilt. Plez didn't raise cotton this year and I can't ask Pa. He was so dead set against my marrying Plez. I haven't seen him since we ran off and got married. I hear from my brothers and Ida that he hasn't changed his mind. And Ma just cries all the time."

The two young women sat on a heap of cotton in a shed on the McMasters farmstead. Everett McMasters kept his seeds after the cotton gin separated them during the ginning process. Tufts of cotton clung to the seeds and the girls pulled the cotton from the seeds and strung it across the cards. They threw the seeds in a bucket to save them for animal feed.

Flora concentrated on filling one of the cards with cotton. She dropped the seeds in her lap. "I'm going to crack and eat a few seeds while I rest," she said. "I just love them."

Esther laughed and reached into the bucket for a handful of seeds. "I don't have any saved up so I'll just have to replace these," she said as she popped one into her mouth and cracked it. Spitting out the seed into her hand, she threw the hull back into the bucket and ate the seed. "Pa saves hulls and all for feed," she said, "so I guess we'll have to drop seeds in our laps if we want to eat any more."

She ate several more seeds before she said, "I know it must be terribly sad at your folks' place. I can't imagine what it would be like to lose a brother."

Flora stifled a sob as her eyes brimmed with tears. Esther moved to sit beside her and put her arms around her. Tears spilled down Flora's cheeks and her body shook.

"It's been hard on me, too, but I have Plez. My family doesn't understand, but I couldn't face this loss without the man I love. Pa never would have consented to my marrying him, but it was the only thing I could do. I do feel so bad for my folks. If you look at it one way, they have lost three children. They haven't heard from Buford since he left. If it were up to me, I'd make up with them in a minute. Plez feels the same way. Paul was his best friend." Sobs overtook her and she buried her face in her hands.

Esther cast about in her mind for a way to comfort her friend. She stroked Flora's shoulder until the weeping subsided, then asked, "How is the rest of the family holding up?"

"The little ones seem to be fine, if I can trust what Jed tells me. You know Jed; he's always so happy-go-lucky. But I feel like he forces himself now to put the best face on things. So when he tells me Pa and Ma are having a bad time I know it is probably worse than he says. And Ben goes along just like he always has; he's carrying a bigger load, of course, with the two older boys gone." She hesitated. Esther knew her friend so well that she expected Flora to say more. But Flora grabbed a handful of cotton and began tearing it apart, dropping the seeds in the bucket and the cotton in her lap.

Esther prompted her. "Were you going to say something else?"

Flora said, "I don't know whether I should tell you this or not. I've been mulling it over and I think you should know. I'm sure my brother Ben has fallen for you. I could see it in his eyes the night of the birthday party. When Jed walked in and it was so obvious that you two were sweethearts, Ben looked like a boulder had flattened him. He'll never say or do anything to come between you and Jed, but I love my brother and I can't stand to see him hurt. I know you would never do anything intentionally to hurt a fly so, I thought, if you knew, you could be gentle with Ben."

The news shocked Esther. She had hardly exchanged two words with Ben. The only time she had even seen him when Jed hadn't been present was that short time at the party before Jed arrived. "Are you sure?" she asked.

"I'm as sure as I know that we're sitting here carding cotton. I know Ben like a book. We've been like that"—she raised her hand with index and middle finger appearing to be glued together—"all my life. I'd stake my life on it."

The revelation had worried Esther ever since. She loved Jed Conover with all her heart and had never looked at another man. Many other boys had come calling since she entered her teens but her father and brothers protected her ferociously. It was like they packed me in cotton batting, she thought. At times she felt smothered but she had set high standards for any suitor. First of all, he must be a Christian. The church meant as much to her as it did to her father. She had a hard time understanding some of the ways her brothers acted. The two older ones played their music in saloons, for instance. She didn't understand why her Pa tolerated it. It was all right to perform on stage or at play parties where parents and chaperones allowed no foolishness. In those locations, too, Beulah could play with them.

Then, any man she cared about must be honest and truthful. She would countenance no underhandedness of any sort. He must be aboveboard in every way. More than once she had known men who pretended to be Christians that turned out to be two-faced. Double-minded was what the Bible called it.

When Jed moved to Indian Territory nearly a year ago, she knew at once she had found the man of her dreams. Not only did he have all the inner qualities she desired; he was the most handsome man she had ever seen. He was so much fun to be with, too. Even before they had paired off, when a crowd got together, he kept them all in stitches with the way he turned any gathering into a good time.

At first she thought he didn't meet all her requirements, but before long he started to attend church. She knew the Conover family believed the way she did because Flora had told her. In fact, that was one reason she and Flora were such good friends; they had met at church the first Sunday after the Conover family moved there.

Just then she heard a knock on the door and Flora walked on in as she customarily did. She carried a quilt top and lining as well as thread and needles.

"Come on in," Esther said. "Steady this chair for me while I tie these cords in the staples in the ceiling. I just found the twine and big needles to sew the lining in the frames. When we get the frames swung, Ma will help us put the quilt in. Let me see which top you brought."

Flora folded back a corner of the quilt displaying a patchwork block with a name embroidered in a long rectangle in the center.

"Oh, good. I was hoping you would choose your friendship quilt. You'll want it quilted by the piece, won't you? You know what we ought to do is make everybody quilt their own block. That way you can see what kind of hand they are to quilt."

"You just say that because you know you'll show off how well you quilt. Not many ladies in the country can beat you. Sister Goodgion, of course, and your mother and maybe mine. Do you have any idea whether Ma will try to come?" Flora had tears in her eyes. "It won't feel right to have my quilting bee without her."

Tears welled in Esther's eyes in sympathy with her friend. "I don't know, Essie. We invited her and Ida. I think Ida will be here because she doesn't like to miss any kind of gathering even if there is work involved. But I just don't know about your Ma."

She picked up one end of a short quilting frame and inserted it in a loop at the end of one of the strings hanging from the ceiling. Flora grabbed the other end and placed it in the loop of another string suspending the frame about thirty inches from the floor. Working together, the two friends swung the other short frame and laid the longer pieces across them fastening them by dropping large nails through holes near the corners. Then, using large needles threaded with twine, they attached the lining to the frames by looping the twine around the frame between stitches in the lining.

Scarcely had they finished their task when they heard the sound of hoofbeats and ran to look out the door. "Look at all the buggies and traps," Esther said. "They must have met somewhere and come in a body." She ran to meet the first buggy at the same time her brothers arrived from the barn.

"Don't worry about your animals, ladies," Claude told them. "We'll take good care of them today for you."

As she watched small children run to play in the yard, Esther called to the arriving women, "Come on in, we've just been wishing for someone with long arms to place the batts in the middle of the quilt."

Laughing, Polly Wilson pushed Abby McIntosh forward. Esther felt sorry for the woman because she could see her embarrassment. Abby had never before attended any of the gatherings of the neighborhood women. Esther knew she was shy and believed she had come this day only because Flora was now kin to her. But Abby handed her baby to Polly and followed Esther and Flora into the house.

The ladies followed Judith McMasters to the kitchen with their contribution to lunch and then settled to work. Many hands made quick work of spreading the batts and covering them with the top. Esther explained her idea of each one quilting her own block. "That way if Plez hangs his toe in a stitch, they'll know who caused the tragedy," she said.

A knock on the door announced Lillie and Ida Conover. Ida bounced in, stating, "We decided to walk; it's such a nice morning. Betsy has already found her friends and started to play." She leaned over the quilt and groaned. "Oh, no, you're quilting by the piece. I'm going out in the yard and play with the little kids."

Esther could have hugged her for breaking the ice. Flora did hug her and studied her mother as she did so. On Sundays since Flora and Plez had returned from their wedding trip, Lillie had made it a point to speak formally to them at church. But Lillie must have decided to end their estrangement because she held out her arms and Flora ran into them. The room got real quiet until Prudence Goodgion said, "Judith, pitch me the thread, will you. Ida, you sit down here by me and I'll help you. Did you bring your thimble and needle?"

Taking her cue, all the other women began chattering again.

Esther said to Flora, "I know your Ma is tired from her walk. You two go sit on the porch and I'll bring you a cool drink."

After the noon meal, the ladies and older girls settled to their task of finishing the quilt. Esther's idea of each quilting her own block had not worked out exactly as she had planned because Flora wanted to quilt although she had not made a block of the friendship quilt. Too, some of the block makers did not attend the bee. Companionship and lighthearted teasing had contributed to a fun-filled day. Ida broke her second needle of the day and one of the ladies offered her a large sack needle. The room rang with laughter.

Just then, the back door banged as Beulah came home from school. She barged in holding a piece of paper aloft. "Essie," she squealed, "I found a letter for you from your sweetheart. It was in a hole in a tree. I couldn't imagine what it was so I read it and brought it to you. Oh, I forgot you can't read. Here, I'll read it to you. 'Dear Esther, I don't know how to tell you this.'"

Esther knocked her chair over as she arose hastily, reaching for the note. Beulah danced out of her reach and ran around the quilt, reading as she ran. "'By the time you get this, Vinnie Wade and I will be married.'"

Indrawn breaths sounded in unison from everyone in the room. Esther still chased her sister but hadn't caught her when Beulah reached Ida's chair. The girl grabbed her and held her arm while Esther pried the note from her grasp.

Esther, white as the paper she held, stood as if rooted to the spot while the air quivered in the hushed room. She heard Prudence

Goodgion say, "Sisters, I think a prayer might be useful here." She bowed her head and began to pray.

When all heads were bowed, Esther took the opportunity to slip into the room her brothers shared. She wished she could collapse on her own bed, but she and Beulah shared a bed in the front room where the quilters worked. She folded the note and held it at arm's length as if it were a poisonous snake. The words Beulah had read burned in her mind and she felt they were making a black hole in her heart. Charred around the edges, burnt and crisp, they scratched and dug at her insides.

She didn't know how long she stood rigid until her arm began to ache from the unnatural position. It dropped to her side as if of its own accord and the paper fluttered to the floor. Stooping to retrieve it, she noticed the long rectangle of sunlight cast by the westering sun shining through the uncurtained window. How can that be, she thought. The sun is still high and a lifetime has passed since I heard this unbearable news. It can't be true; Beulah is playing a terrible trick on me.

Sitting on the bed, she unfolded the note and smoothed it with trembling fingers. Written in pencil on lined stationery, the words seemed to leap out at her.

∽

"Dear Esther,

"I do not know how to tell you this. By the time you get this, Vinnie Wade and I will be married. I cannot explain nor will I try. But know this: YOU are the one I love.

"Jed"

She read it again and again and finally the truth of the message seeped into her conscious mind. It doesn't make sense, she thought. Time and time again in the past month since Flora and Plez had married, Jed had begged her to run away with him. Even Flora had tried to influence her. "We'd be sisters-in-law," she had said. "We feel more like sisters to each other now than we do to our own sisters."

But Esther had refused to lie about her age and she knew her father would never sign for her to marry Jed. For a reason incomprehensible to Esther, her father had reservations about the relationship.

She lay back across the bed and folded her hands at her waist over the letter. The words echoed in her head until only the last sentence repeated like a scratched phonograph record. In spite of the mortal blow dealt by the rest of the missive, she hugged those words to her heart. She imagined she heard them from his own lips in his deep voice and that she felt the rough homespun of his shirt on her cheek and the warmth of his encircling arms.

Warm tears brimmed in her eyes and she rolled over and buried her face in the soft quilt covering the bed and let the cleansing flood spill. She had no idea how long she had lain thus when she heard the springs creak and felt a weight on the mattress as someone sat and began patting her shoulder. She gulped and swallowed as Flora thrust a handkerchief into her hand and said, "Here, wipe your eyes."

Esther's first thought concerned the note. When the weeping overwhelmed her and she flipped onto her stomach, she had paid no attention to its location. Though Beulah no doubt knew its contents, the words had become alive to Esther and she did not want anyone else to see them. Even Flora, she thought. This news makes me feel naked. No, worse, naked and bludgeoned black and blue. I can't share this feeling with anyone including my best friend.

She let Flora help her sit up and used the proffered handkerchief. When her eyes cleared enough to see, she found the crumpled paper where she had lain on it. Picking it up, she pressed out the wrinkles with her fingers, folded it and put it in her pocket.

Flora said, "We've finished the quilt. Some of the ladies are taking it out of the frames now. Your mother asked me to come in and see if you think you are ready to come out and bid your guests good-bye."

She paused and looked helplessly at Esther. "There," she continued, "I've delivered her message. Oh, Essie, I don't see how you can bear to go back out there and face all those curious eyes. They are concerned about you, but you know the minute they get out of earshot they'll start talking. What is your Ma *thinking*!"

Esther let the words sink in and thought; I wonder how I feel. Her mind and body refused to feel any emotion. I feel numb, she thought.

"Today is Thursday," she said. "I'll be in church come Sunday and see a lot of them then." She sighed. "Could you bring me a wet washcloth? I'll wash my face and redd up my hair. Then if you'll stand beside me and give me support, I think I can walk out that door and face the mob."

CHAPTER 23

Lillie

Lillie's heart began pounding at the first words of Jed's note. Deep foreboding settled over her like a suffocating blanket. Jed had not been acting like himself this past month or two. His quick wit hardly ever surfaced and the light banter he had always carried on with Ben seemed a thing of the past even though Ben tried to provoke him. As Beulah read the announcement of his elopement, she fought for breath and thought she would faint. When the ladies bowed their heads to pray and she watched Esther escape, she stumbled to the porch and leaned against a post gasping for breath.

Flora followed her outside. "Ma, can I get you anything?" she asked.

She opened her eyes and looked at the distraught expression on her daughter's face. She's afraid I'm going to have one of my spells, she thought, and offered a silent prayer for strength. "Yes," she said, "get me a drink of water and a cloth to bathe my face."

Flora looked afraid to leave her. "No, no, go on," Lillie said. "I'll be all right. I'll just sit here in the porch swing until you get back."

She felt a little better after she washed her face. "Go tell Ida to round up Betsy, please," she said. "I think we'll head home."

"Ma, are you sure you feel like walking? I can go get our buggy and take you. It's just across the road," Flora said.

"No, the walk will do me good. Apologize to Mrs. McMasters for me, too, please. I don't think I can go back in there. I'm going to start on home. Ida and Betsy can come later."

The girls didn't catch up with her before she got home. Lillie appreciated the breather. Her mind refused to accept the import of the message she had heard. And, yet, it must be true, else why would Jed wound Esther in such a way? She had so many questions and didn't know who could answer them.

When she turned into the lane leading up to their house, she saw Holt running to meet her. "Ma, Ma, wait till you hear what happened today!" He was breathless with excitement.

Lillie put her arm around the boy's shoulders and murmured, "Yes, Holt, I heard."

But he couldn't contain his recital of the news. "Mr. Wade came after Jed with his shot gun and Jed had to go marry Vinnie Wade!"

Lillie stopped stock still in the middle of the lane and put her hands on Holt's shoulders. Never in her life had she shook one of her children but she had a strong urge to shake Holt. "Don't you ever say such a thing again," she said. "Where did you hear a story like that?"

Abashed, Holt said, "Part of it at school and part Ben told me. Hezzie Hathcock came to school and told everybody that his Grandpa Wade was going after Jed with his shotgun. I tried to hush him up but he just yelled louder. When I got home, Jed was gone and I asked Ben about it. Ben told me that Jed and Pa left for town so Pa could sign for Jed to get married. I asked him, 'Who to?' and he said, 'Vinnie Wade.' So I guess Hezzie told the truth, after all."

Lillie felt compassion for Holt and, as she thought about it, for her other sons, too. As Jed's note began to make sense to her, she felt heartsick. How had these children of hers gone so wrong is a period of a few weeks? She placed her arm across Holt's shoulders and they walked slowly home.

Ida and Betsy soon arrived with Matt, riding Spot, not far behind them. Lillie watched him slowly unsaddle the horse. His movements reminded her of someone walking in waist-deep water. Every movement required effort. When he trudged toward the house, she said to her children, "I want to talk to your Pa alone. Go find something to do outside. And don't come back till I call you." They scattered like a flock of hens scared by a hawk.

Busying herself at the range, she blew on the smoldering coals and added shavings until she had a blaze, arranged kindling and short sticks of firewood to make a hot fire. Dipping water into her new percolator, she set it over the open flame, measured coffee grounds into the basket and snapped the lid in place.

Matt came in the back door and hung his hat on a peg. Without a word he crossed to his favorite chair and slumped in it.

Lillie tried to present a calm appearance as she waited impatiently for the coffee to brew. When Matt was in a black mood like this, she usually left him alone to stew. But she had to know the straight account of the day's events. Buford had already disgraced the family but, out of sympathy for Paul's death, no one had shunned them because of it. But Jed's shameful affair, if true, threatened their standing in a newfound community, to say nothing of the mortification family members felt over it.

Coffee gurgled as it hit the glass top of the lid and fell over the grounds. Lillie got out Matt's mustache cup, a cup for herself and two saucers. Going to the bay window, she skimmed cream into a small pitcher and carried it all to the table. "Matt, come drink a cup of coffee with me," she said.

He pushed out of the chair and reached the table in two steps. Dragging a dining chair back from the table, he sat and stared at his cup as she filled it with steaming coffee. After she sat and creamed her coffee, she pushed the pitcher to him. As if in a dream, he pulled his chair close to the table, poured cream into his cup, got a spoon from the holder in the middle of the table, and stirred slowly.

Impatience got the better of her. "Well?" she said.

"I don't want to talk about it."

Anger flew all over her. She had let them get by with shielding her for so long that it had built and built until now it overflowed in a rush. "Well, you *will* talk about it," she said. "I intend to know everything that has gone on this day, and you're the one that's going to tell me."

He had been in the process of pouring hot coffee into his saucer. Her tirade startled him so that he splashed it onto the table. She jumped up and grabbed a cloth to blot the puddle before it ran onto the floor. Seeing his distress, she decided to take a different approach.

"Matt, I know that this morning I left here with things not right between us. I'm sorry. I explained my reasons then but I hope you'll listen again. We've allowed our oldest daughter's marriage to stand although we could have had it annulled. With that in mind, I felt I couldn't allow her special quilt to be finished without a stitch from me in it. It's something she will keep all her life and probably pass it down to a daughter if she has one. Matt, I'll tell you how much it means to her. She even had little Betsy put some stitches in it."

Remembrance of Betsy's stitches made her smile. "You should have seen them. Even though I guided her little hand, the stitches came out about an inch long. Matt, you don't understand how much things like this mean to women. Please forgive me for defying you and going anyway."

His piercing blue eyes softened and he reached across the table to take her hand. "My little Lillie," he said. "I've been too hard on you about this. I still can't bring myself to accept her marriage but I know you're seeing her at church and I'll try not to stand in your way. I'm not ready to see her yet but that's the least of my worries right now."

She squeezed his hand and got up to get them more coffee. With her back to him, she said, "Tell me what happened today."

He didn't answer right away. She poured his coffee; he creamed it and tipped a little into his saucer. Holding the saucer in both hands, he lifted it to his lips and blew on it to cool it. After tasting it for temperature, he swallowed the coffee.

He was in the process of pouring more coffee into his saucer when Lillie's impatience spilled over. "Matt," she said. "Tell me."

"Hiram Wade came after Jed with his shotgun," he said.

Lillie gasped.

Matt amended his stark statement. "He didn't actually pull the gun and point it at Jed, but it's the same thing. I could see he meant business. Ben and Jed saw it, too. I convinced Wade that if he would go on home that I would bring Jed over there and we would get things straightened out.

"I made Jed clean up and we went over there. Jed cried and begged me not to make him go. But I had given Wade my word. I did let Jed leave a note for Esther although I don't know what good it did. The way it turned out, the four of us went for the license and then Wade and I were witnesses to the marriage. I had to sign for Jed but the Wade girl is of age."

Bare bones, Lillie thought. That's all I'm going to hear from him. No details. No emotion. His voice sounds dead, almost like he's reading a newspaper account of the marriage of a distant acquaintance. Tears filled her eyes and spilled down her cheeks. I don't know whom I'm crying for, she thought, for Matt or Jed or myself.

"Where are they going to live?"

"At the Wade's. Jed took his clothes, his horse, and his gun with him when he left."

Matt moved from the table back to his chair. Subject closed, Lillie thought as she rose to prepare supper.

CHAPTER 24

Ben

Ben felt two ways about his brother's marriage. Feeling sorry for Jed didn't begin to express his deep regret for the circumstances. He had suspected something like this and, in the few weeks since Vinnie Wade crashed the party, he had made discreet inquiries about her. People seemed to know little about the girl herself, but gossiped freely about the family's reputation. The father raised good enough crops but could have done much better if he'd cleaned out the weeds and grass. He had no sons and word had it that he beat his daughters to make them work in the fields along with him. The two oldest girls had gotten in trouble and he made the boys marry them. As a result, his family had increased with the sons-in-law and the raggedy kids all living with him.

Ben worried about Jed's living in those conditions. But he surely didn't want the two of them living with his family. Jed's wife would never fit in. Jed was a good hand to work. It would be better if he could hire out to some farmer. But this time of year, no one was hiring.

On the other hand, Jed's marriage meant that Esther was now free. Although Ben doubted he stood a chance with her, he couldn't quash a faint ray of hope. He saw her at times, once when it rained while his mother and the girls were at church and he rode his horse there so he could drive the buggy home for them. Twice he found her at Flora's when he delivered a loaf of bread or some other offering his mother sent. She looked like the light had gone out leaving her in the dark. Her pale skin had taken on a gray tinge and her black hair had lost its luster. She took part in conversation but obviously her thoughts were elsewhere. He thought, give her a year to grieve. And, Lord, give me patience. For Ben, it was about as much praying as he ever did.

In the meantime, work overwhelmed him. Instead of five men to do the heavy work, the number had dropped to two. You might as well say one or one and a half. Pa spent a lot of time in his chair; some mornings he stayed in bed until after sunup. When Ben asked him for instructions for the day's work, he said, "Whatever needs doing," or "You're a grown man. It's time you learned to lay out the work."

In a way, Ben liked the challenge. Farming his own land had been his dream all his life. But he had planned to buy a few acres in Texas. He had saved his money for a particular place he had his eye on. Now any thought of returning to his home state seemed a distant dream. He thought, give it up. Think of Esther; she's worth any sacrifice. He made a special trip to town and had the money transferred from the Texas bank.

Winter came on fast. Or so it seemed. Spring had been late that year and that threw harvest two or three weeks later than usual. As a result, a good deal of the cotton bolls remained unopened. They harvested all they could then turned their attention to the corn they had let dry on the stalks. With the crib full of corn and cottonseed heaped in a stall, Ben felt secure of feed for the animals.

That morning he tried again to find out what his father wanted done. Last year they had cut down trees and pulled stumps to add acreage for crops. He needed to harvest the sweet potatoes from that area and prepare it for spring plowing. Pecans were beginning to fall.

Ma and the kids could pick up those in the yard but he would have to flail them. Two things he wanted to ask their landlord but he hated to go over Pa's head. If Pa wanted to add more cropland this year, would Mr. McIntosh want to decide the location of the trees to cut down? And could they pick up his pecans on the halves?

When he went to look for his father, he found him in bed with the curtains drawn. Ben thought he wasn't asleep because his eyelids fluttered the least bit. He stood beside the bed undecided for a minute, then took a chance on Pa's anger. Truth to tell, he wished Pa would get angry—anything but the dull, uncaring way he acted lately.

Ben felt and heard the springs creak as he plopped down on the bed. Matt opened his eyes and looked at his son with a listless stare.

"Pa, we have to talk about the work. So many jobs stare me in the face that I don't know where to start. If you don't feel like it, you don't need to help with the actual work, just tell me what you want me to do and I'll do it."

Matt stirred and sat up in bed, stacked Lillie's pillow on top of his, and leaned back. His face looked like a wood cut, set and unexpressive; his head pulled to one side as if his neck were too weak to hold it up. With an effort, he said, "Son, you know the work as well as I do. What do you want from me?"

Ben considered his father's question. True, he had worked side by side with Pa since he was a little shaver. But Pa was so old-fashioned. He refused to try new ways of doing things. Ben ached to innovate, to put new methods to the test. Only, in his present state of mind, would it be right to mention anything like that to Pa? He decided against it. Instead, he said, "We need to ask Stump where he wants us to cut trees this year. And I'd like to try to pick up pecans on his land. I don't know what he'd think if I talked to him; wouldn't it be better for you to do it?"

"If you tell him I sent you, it'll be all right. Go ahead and see him for me." Matt prepared to lie back down.

"Pa, don't you feel like getting up this morning? Ma taught Ida to make flapjacks. She's making a good cook, believe it or not. I think she would feel good about it if you tried some and told her how good they are."

Matt closed his eyes. Disappointed, Ben left the room. When the door swung on well-oiled hinges, he toyed with slamming the door to show his frustration but didn't dare.

Betsy ran to him and took his hand. "My Pa's sick, Ben," she said, beginning to cry.

Ben picked her up and hugged her. Hoping his father would hear him, he made no effort to lower his voice when he said, "Yes, Honey, Pa's sick. So we have to help him by doing his share of the work. I think Ma and Ida are picking up pecans. Put on your old coat and go help them."

He set her down, helped her find a coat, and led her outside. "Go help Ma," he said. "I want to talk to Ida."

He walked across the yard to the tree where Ida knelt harvesting pecans. Squatting beside her, he surveyed the number of nuts that had fallen. "Ida, if I frail these trees, do you think you can help me on the two-man saw when I chop down some trees for firewood?"

Ida rocked back into a sitting position. "You know I don't know how to use that saw. Can it wait until Holt gets in from school?"

"I don't think he's strong enough to pull his side. I can teach you. Come on, Ide, you know we have to work together now that all the other boys are gone and Pa is sick."

Tears formed in Ida's eyes. She dashed them away with a quick flutter of her hand. "I don't think Pa is sick. I don't know what's wrong with him, but he would be strong enough if he would just eat."

"I know. I told him how good your flapjacks were this morning and tried to get him up to eat, but he just shut his eyes. Sis, you're getting to be a good cook." Compliments had never come easy to Ben's lips and he ducked his head so that he didn't see Ida's reaction.

She blushed and touched his hand. "I tell you what. You get the frail pole and I'll go cook some sausage and pancakes. Maybe smelling the sausage will make him hungry."

"Make me a couple of sausage sandwiches to take with me to the wood lot. I'll chop down what trees I can today and we'll see about sawing them up later."

In the grove of blackjack and post oak trees that their landlord had set aside for them to use as a woodlot, Ben attacked the base of a blackjack with a double-bit axe. At first he worked with all the fury he felt at the events of the morning. But soon he settled into a steady rhythm of getting set, striking the tree, feeling the axe bite into the wood and bounce back, pulling the tool back over his shoulder, and aiming the axe to cut out a chip. Over and over, he repeated the action until he had a gash on one side of the tree, then chopped on the other side until the tree leaned into the gash and fell.

He had started on the third tree when he had the eerie feeling that someone was watching him. Cautiously turning his head, he saw his brother-in-law grinning at him. "How did you get here?" he asked. "I didn't hear you come up."

"Guess it's a habit to walk without making any racket," Plez said. "I heard chopping down here and thought you might could use some help."

Ben noticed the single-bit axe leaning beside Plez's leg. "Man, that would be welcome. But don't you have your own work? I thought you were building a house."

"That can wait. Flora sent me. She's worried about her family getting cold this winter. What do you want me to do?"

"How about chopping the small limbs off the trees I've already cut? I'll move to another tree for the time being so I can make it fall away from you."

The two men worked throughout the morning. When the sun approached its zenith, Ben invited Plez to share his lunch.

"You don't think Flora would send me off without something to eat, do you?" Plez said. "I brought my own dinner, but I'm ready to rest awhile."

Plez finished a biscuit sandwich before he said, "Have you heard that Uncle Stump wants to sell out here and move back to southeastern Oklahoma?"

Ben's throat felt dry. That meant the pecan grove might be for sale. "No, this is the first I've heard about it," he said. "I'm surprised he wants to leave. He appeared to me to be pretty settled here."

"He came to talk to Pa and me about it last night. He says Abby has been torn up ever since Paul was killed almost in her front yard. She doesn't have any people here and she wants to move back close to her folks. And, then, too, since Oklahoma came in as a dry state, Unc feels uneasy about his business. Of course, Chickasaw Nation was dry, too, but he was used to dealing with their lawmen. Now, everything has changed and he thinks that with the money from selling out, he can make a go of something down there near her folks."

Ben had been only half listening. His mind raced with questions. Would Stump divide up the land so that he could have a chance to buy a part of it? He knew he didn't have enough money saved to purchase very many acres. Would the bank loan him the rest? After all, he was new here and young. But he was of age and could handle his own business. When Plez stopped for breath, he shot him another question; "Does he have a buyer?"

"He plans to give your Pa first chance since he is already established. Do you think he will be interested?"

"Plez, I don't know. Do you realize how much Pa has gone down since everything that has happened this fall? I don't know whether he can talk business or not. He told me this morning to talk to Mr. McIntosh about picking up pecans and clearing more land."

Plez bit into another biscuit and waited for Ben to continue. Ben refolded a pancake over a sausage patty and chewed slowly as he considered the possibilities of owning his own land. "I know Pa has money from the sale of his Pa's hundred-sixty-acre homestead in Texas. I don't know how much he got; he has never let anyone in on his business. How many acres will be up for sale?"

Plez said, "He got three allotments—one for him, one for Abby, and one for Ray. The rolls had already been closed before the baby was born. He took one quarter in the section with ours. My Pa's thinking about buying it. So he'll have half of this section for sale, three hundred twenty acres."

Ben took the last bite of his lunch. "I'd like to go talk to him now if he's home. Do you know?"

"I saw him when I passed by his house on the way here. I guess you'd just have to go over there to see if he's still there."

"Would you go with me?"

"I think I'll stay here and finish trimming up these trees. You can tell him I told you about the land."

Ben left his axe leaning against a tree. "I'll come back this way today and get it," he told Plez. "I'm much obliged for all the help you've been to me today." He shook his brother-in-law's hand.

When he knocked on the McIntosh's door, Stump opened it and stepped outside. "Pardon me for not inviting you in," he said. "Abby doesn't feel like seeing anybody today." He led Ben to a couple of stumps in the yard.

Ben cast about in his mind for the best way to broach the subject of purchasing the land.

McIntosh continued, "The constable just left here. He brought a subpoena for Abby to appear at a hearing in Ardmore. They caught the Sexton boys in Texas and brought them back to the county jail. Abby's scared to death to testify. Has your Pa got a notice?"

Elation at the news of the Sextons' capture fought with uneasiness that Buford also had been found. He decided to wait and see if any news about Buford was forthcoming. "I haven't been home since this morning," he said. "Did he say he was going to see Pa?"

"He didn't say one way or the other." When Ben remained silent, McIntosh said, "What can I do for you?"

Ben still hadn't figured out the best way to approach the man about buying his property. Instead, he said, "Pa asked me to come see you for him. He's been under the weather lately. We wanted to know what land you want us to clear this year. And I'd like to make arrangements to pick up pecans on shares unless you have already made other arrangements."

"Tell you the truth, Ben, things are pretty much up in the air right now. I'm thinking about selling my land and moving back closer to Abby's family. But this notice for her to appear in court has us both upset. I was intending to go see your Pa today to see if he wanted to buy this place but I'd better not leave her alone."

"Plez mentioned something to me about your plans. I don't know how much land Pa would want to buy, but I'd like to talk to you about part of it if you would split it up. I don't want to run under Pa, though, so let me talk to him about it and see what we can work out. Would that be all right with you?"

Stump seemed to consider the question. "Yes, that would be all right. Tell him that my mind is pretty well made up. But this trial will slow me down some. I don't know how long it will take, but we don't have to be in any hurry on the real estate deal. We can go on the way we have been doing until we work something out."

"That sounds good enough to me. Just one thing, will you give us first chance?"

"Yes. You have my word on that."

The two men shook hands and Ben left for home. When he walked through the wood lot to retrieve his axe, he saw that Plez had finished trimming the trees they had cut that morning. Squinting at the sun, he judged it to be three hours high. He wondered how Pa would react to getting a subpoena and felt torn between being with him to soften the news and letting him alone to see how he would handle it. But he wanted to have as many trees ready to saw to length as he could when he moved the cradles and crosscut saw to the area. Instead of heading home immediately, he decided to cut another tree or two.

CHAPTER 25

Lillie

After Ida went into the house to prepare a tempting breakfast for Matt, Lillie drew Betsy away from the pecan trees while Ben flailed them.

"There, Ma," Ben said as he walked toward them. "I just gave the trees a lick and a promise, but I want to get some wood cut. We have plenty of wood for the cook stove but it'll go down fast when we have to start burning more for heat." He put one arm around Lillie and gave her a peck on the cheek. "I promise to do a better job after some more shucks open."

"It looks like the ground is covered," Lillie said. "We'll have plenty work for today, won't we, Betsy? Thank you, Son." She gave Ben a quick hug.

Betsy held up her arms and Ben lifted her above his head then let her fall, caught her on the way down, and gave her a mock squeeze. She yelled and giggled. Putting her down, he said, "I'll go see if Ida has my dinner fixed and get my axe and get going."

She and Betsy began plucking nuts from the clean-swept yard and dropping them into syrup buckets. Betsy loved the plink-plink of nuts hitting metal buckets. She scrambled after more nuts, her small nimble fingers snatching them quickly. She has a good eye, Lillie thought, but she'll tire soon.

Ida joined them. Lillie raised her eyebrows in a silent question.

Ida smiled. "I fixed him a plate and took it to the bed and waved it close to his nose. I said, 'If you're able to sit up, maybe you can eat a few bites. I'll go get you some coffee.' I could tell it made him mad but it got him going."

She knelt beside her mother, collected a handful of pecans, and deposited them in her bucket. "He said, 'Being as you've gone to all this trouble, I'll get up and come to the table.' Of course, that was just what I wanted him to do. So I waited on him while he ate and then I cleaned up the dishes."

"So what did he do after he ate? How much did he eat?" Lillie's anxiety spilled over.

"He ate about half a plateful, drank all his coffee, and then went and sat down in his big chair and put his feet up."

Lillie sighed. "Well, that's better than he did yesterday. I wish we could think of something to do that would bring him out of it. Poor Ben is working his fingers to the bone without any help and not complaining. There's so much work to do and so few hands to do it. We need to get as much accomplished as we can while this good weather holds."

The woman and two girls worked quietly until Lillie heard Betsy cracking a pecan with her teeth. "Are you getting hungry?" she asked the child. "I tell you what. Go down in the dugout and get four apples—can you count to four?" Betsy shook her head. Lillie handed her four pecans. "Get one for each pecan," she said. "Take one for your Pa and ask him to peel mine for me."

Betsy ran toward the dugout. "Wash your hands first," Lillie cried after her. "Carry the apples in your apron so you won't drop them."

"Has Pa ever asked where we got the apples?" Ida said.

"No. And that's another curious thing. When he was at himself, he kept up with every little detail. I wonder if he guessed that Flora gave us the apples and decided not to bring it up. Maybe I'm just hoping, but I think he may be starting to be sorry he passed such harsh judgment on her and Plez."

Ida shook her head. "I don't know what has gotten into him. He was moody before Jed got married, but ever since then he has withdrawn into himself. He shakes it part of the time and does pretty well. Is he still going to the graveyard every day?"

"He never mentions it, but I'm sure he does. He gives the excuse of exercising Paul's horse. Or sometimes he walks when the weather is fine like it is today. Ida, I don't want you to ever say anything to him about it. I went through the same thing when Terence died. Taking care of Ben finally brought me out of it, although I still had spells for a while afterwards. But I know I'm cured now and I'm sure that Matt will be well again." She sighed. "I just don't know how long it will take nor what process we'll all have to go through in the meantime."

Betsy came running from the house with a peeled apple held aloft and the others clutched in a pouch made by grasping her apron in the other hand. "Pa didn't want an apple," she said. "He said he'd just had breakfast."

"We'll go ahead and eat then," Lillie said. "We can crack our pecans using a rock against the back step. Ida, you draw a bucket of fresh water. We'll have apples and pecans and cool water for our meal. We won't disturb your Pa."

Lillie had a hard time keeping Betsy working and finally decided to let her go into the house. She had two minds about disturbing Matt, anyway. Maybe Betsy would have more success at bringing him out of his doldrums than anyone else. The child had a way about her that usually proved irresistible.

About two o'clock she heard sounds of a horse coming down the lane. Pushing to an upright position she brushed the dirt from her skirt with her hands as well as she could, washed her hands at the wash stand, and smoothed her hair. She didn't recognize the horseman.

He tipped his hat and said, "Howdy, Ma'am." He nodded courteously to Ida who had walked to Lillie's side.

"Sir," Lillie said.

"I'm looking for the Matthew Conover place. Have I found it?"

"Yes."

"Is Mr. Conover to home?"

Lillie turned to Ida, "Go ask your Pa to come out here," she said.

Matt appeared shortly, Ida right behind him and Betsy leading the way. Lillie put out her hand and corralled her as she passed.

"Evening," Matt said to the horseman. "Won't you get down and come in?"

The man alighted from his horse. "Let me introduce myself," he said. "Name's Gib Stallworth. I'm here on some business, Mr. Conover. You are Matthew Conover?"

"Yes, of course. If this is private, come on in the house." He spoke to Ida. "Draw a bucket of fresh water, please, Ida, so Mr. Stallworth can have a cool drink."

Lillie watched as Matt opened the door and stood aside for Stallworth to precede him. Ida poured the remaining water from the bucket by the back door into the large wash pan and drew water from the well. "Here, I'll take it in to them." Lillie reached for the bucket. She could tell that Ida handed over the water reluctantly. She's as curious as I am, Lillie thought, but I'll be less intrusive.

Just as she entered the room, Stallworth handed Matt a paper. Matt sat staring at it a few minutes before he unfolded it. Lillie set the water pail on the cabinet and filled a glass for the visitor. She had started to go back out the door when Matt stopped her.

"Stallworth here has brought us some news. They've captured the Sexton boys. They have them over at Ardmore in the county jail. This paper is a subpoena for me to appear as a witness at their hearing."

Stallworth emptied the glass of water and set it on the table.

Matt looked up from the subpoena. "I've forgotten my manners, Mr. Stallworth. This is my wife, Mrs. Conover. Won't you sit back down and stay a bit?"

Stallworth shuffled his feet and twisted his hat in his hands. "Pleased to meet you, Ma'am," he said. Then, to Matt, "Thank you, no, I've finished my business. I'll be getting on. Thank you, Ma'am, for the drink."

The door had scarcely closed behind him before the two girls burst in wide-eyed with curiosity. They stopped short at the sight of their father's scowl.

Lillie said, "Come on in and hear the news. Then I want you to go finish picking up the pecans while your Pa and I talk." When Matt remained silent, she said, "Would you like to tell them, Matt?"

Matt looked at her as if he weren't sure what she meant. Then he shook his head as if to clear it and said, "Yes. Mr. Stallworth came to tell us that the authorities caught the Sextons in Texas and brought them back. Seems they were trying to cross the border into Mexico. They have them in the county jail."

Ida shouted, "Hallelujah!" but Betsy, looking from Ida's joyful grin to Lillie's worried frown to Matt's tight lips, climbed on her father's lap and tried to pull his mouth into a smile. "Aren't you glad, Papa?" she said.

"Yes, Baby, I'm glad they caught them. But I have a lot of things on my mind right now. You go on outside like your Ma said."

Once they left the room, Matt lapsed into gloom again. "I think I'll fix supper early today," Lillie said. "None of us had much dinner. We'll feel better after a good meal."

Matt appeared not to have heard her, so she built a good fire in the range and left it to settle into coals while she went to get vegetables from the dugout. She scrubbed sweet potatoes before she came back inside, rubbed them with butter and placed a pan full in the oven to bake. After sliding a big pan of cornbread onto another oven shelf, she opened a jar of green beans and dipped kraut from the crock. With the vegetables simmering, she set the table and tried to engage Matt in conversation.

"I'll be so glad when we have a good cold spell so we can kill hogs," she said. "Wouldn't a good mess of fresh pork cutlets taste good right now?"

Matt grunted, so she knew he heard her. Irked, she crossed to his chair and planted herself in front of him. "Matt."

He looked up at her.

"When is the hearing?"

"A week from Monday."

Monosyllables. "I'm going with you." That ought to shake him up.

It did. "Lillie, court is no place for a woman. There's no telling what you might hear. These men are not going to respect you or the court. I can't let you go."

"Matt, Paul's my son the same as yours. I need to be there. I want to see what those murderers look like. I want to be with you when you have to testify, to stand beside you. I think you need me, too."

"I'll be gone at least three days, maybe more. I'll have to spend Sunday night in Ardmore to make the early session. We don't know when they will call this case. It might be several days. Then we have to figure on the best part of a day to get home. I don't think you need to be away from the children that long."

"Ben is a grown man and Ida has grown up a lot lately. They will take care of the other children. Holt is in school now, anyway. Betsy will miss us the most, but she'll be all right." Let him find out after we get back that I'm going to let her go stay with Flora, she thought. "Matt, mull it over and you'll see why I need to go. We'll talk about it again tonight. Now, I think supper is about ready. As soon as Ben gets home, we'll eat."

As soon as Ben raised his head after saying grace, he fastened his gaze on his father and said, "Pa, did you get a subpoena today?"

Surprised, Matt said, "Yes. How did you know?"

Ben split a piece of cornbread, spread butter on it, and passed the butter to Lillie before he answered. "I went over to Stump McIntosh's place today and he told me that Abby had been served with a subpoena."

Ida said, "What were you doing at his place? I thought you had a full day of wood cutting laid out."

Ben hesitated. "I heard that he was thinking about selling out and moving back closer to Abby's folks."

"Where in the world did you hear that?" Ida said.

Lillie guessed that Ben had seen either Flora or Plez and heard the news from them. She said, "Ida, Ida, let Ben tell his news in his own way."

Ben appeared relieved. "Pa," he said, "Stump said he had intended to come over to talk to you about it, but Abby was so perturbed about having to testify that he didn't want to leave her. I got him to promise that he wouldn't sell until he talked to you."

Matt halved a sweet potato and slathered it with butter. Good, Lillie thought, he's eating again.

Slowly, Matt said, "I've got that money from Pa's homestead but it was only a hundred sixty acres. How much of his land does he want to sell?"

"He owns half of this section. I wonder if we could work out some kind of deal so that I buy some of it. I put my savings in the bank in Chagris. Maybe they would talk to me about a loan." His voice showed eagerness that Lillie had not heard from him since before they had begun to talk about leaving Texas. Something has happened to make him change his mind, she thought. I wonder what it is.

Matt said, "Even so, I doubt we can swing the whole deal. Do you think you can take his word for it that he'll hold the land for us?"

Lillie heard the unspoken words, 'After all, he is an Indian and a bootlegger.' She had her doubts, too, but remembering shy Abby's appearance at the quilting bee, she was inclined to believe that family ties mattered to the couple. Matt may be glad someday that he has an Indian son-in-law, she thought.

"Do you think you might ought to go over and see him?" she asked Matt.

Matt said, "Don't hurry me now. We'll sleep on it and see how we feel in the morning."

Lillie had to be satisfied with the answer. Neither did she bring up the subject of accompanying Matt to the hearing. She slept little that night. Matt's involuntary jerking of one leg a couple of times a minute failed to wake him but disturbed her. She had no idea how he would decide the two problems. I must go to the hearing, she thought. What will I do if he puts his foot down and says I can't go?

When she heard the clock strike five, she threw the covers back and put her feet on the cold floor. This time of year, they slept late and Matt had gotten out of his habit of getting up at four o'clock.

He turned over and mumbled, "What time is it?"

"Five," she said. "I'm going to start breakfast and get Ben and Holt up to do the milking."

Matt sat up in bed, yawning. "I'll build your fire for you," he said.

She wanted to jump for joy and shout, "Are you back?" but she only said, "Thank you."

In the kitchen, she said, "Let's let Ida and Betsy sleep until breakfast. It's been a while since Ida hasn't had to get up early."

But Matt said, "No, let Ida help Holt with the milking. I want to talk to you and Ben."

Lillie was afraid to trust her voice to answer. She felt short of breath; did she dare believe that Matt's depression was over? I know it's not, she thought, but I'll enjoy every little chink of light. Slipping into the girls' room, she shook Ida awake. "Your Pa wants you and Holt to milk this morning. Let Betsy sleep until breakfast is ready. I'll cook."

She went to the dugout to wake the boys and found Ben up lighting the lamp. He turned at the sound of her steps, smiled and looked back to fit the chimney inside the prongs. Running to him, she hugged him and whispered, "Your Pa is making the fire and wants Holt and Ida to milk so he can talk to you and me."

Ben caught her arms and danced her around in the narrow space between the beds. "Do you mean it? He's back to his old self?"

"I don't know how long it will last, but let's enjoy it while we can. Get Holt up and come in the kitchen. I'll send Ida out."

Matt's arms rested on the dining table. He stared at his hands as he laced and unlaced his fingers and rubbed his thumbs together. Lillie had seen him in such a pose many times. It meant that he hadn't made up his mind completely but he didn't want anyone else to know that.

"I have to grind the coffee beans," she said. "Go ahead and sit, Ben. You and Matt can talk and I'll listen while I make coffee."

Ben sat across the table from his father and waited. Lillie had her back to them while she worked at the coffee mill. She heard Matt clear his throat.

"I've been considering the proposition of buying land here in Oklahoma," he said. "I don't think any of you, including Lillie, knows why I decided to move up here in the first place."

Lillie was glad he couldn't see her face. He's so transparent, she thought, but he doesn't know it.

But Ben was saying, "I thought it was a strange thing for us to do. But I thought everybody but me was all for it."

"That's another thing that surprises me, Ben. You said you might want to buy some land here. Does that mean that you want to stay?"

"I think I do. If I could get hold of that pecan grove up close to the road west of us, I think I could make something of it."

"So, let me start back at the beginning. The reason I brought my family here in the first place was that Buford was in so much trouble in Texas that I didn't think I could get him out of it. One of my pards in the Rangers let me know that the evidence against him was substantial. Paul had been after me to move, too, so I let him think he had persuaded me."

Lillie set cups and saucers in front of them and poured three cups of coffee. After bringing cream from the bay window, she joined the men.

Matt creamed his coffee and poured some in his saucer to cool. "Here's what I'm thinking. This move up here was probably the worst decision I ever made in my life. It didn't stop Buford's lawlessness and Paul's life was cut short because of it."

Oh, my darling, Lillie thought. Such an admission must have cost you dearly. She put out her hand toward him, but he didn't see her. He had taken his saucer in both hands and brought it to his lips.

Ben looked at her, her pain reflected in his eyes. Neither of them spoke.

Matt poured more coffee into his saucer. "So here's what I've been thinking. Ben, you never intended to stay here. But you're a grown man so that was all right. I'm responsible for the rest of the family. With Buford and Paul gone..." His voice broke and he wiped his eyes with thumb and forefinger. "There's no reason to stay. We can pack up and move back."

"No reason to stay?" Lillie blurted. "No reason to stay? We have two married children here. We can't just move off and leave them."

Matt seemed bewildered by her outburst. "But, Lillie, I thought you would be the first to want to move back. You miss your sisters so much. And that's where your parents and little Terence lie buried."

"My sisters have their own families. I do miss them, but we write to each other. And, Matt, I have a son buried here, too."

"Does that mean you want to stay here?"

"Yes, I do. I'll want to take a trip back to Texas when we can, but here is where I want to make my home."

Matt turned his attention to his son. "Ben, you're still your own man. You can go back if that's your desire. We'll miss you, but I won't try to hold you here."

"No, Pa, I've been giving it some thought lately. With all the other boys gone, you need another hand around the place. I've gone over in my mind the reasons I wanted to stay down there. Not one of them is good enough to build my future on. I can see possibilities in this country. The state is new, the land is fertile, and I think a young man can go places here. I want to stay."

Matt said, "That settles it then. We'll go see Stump today."

CHAPTER 26

Lillie

Sunday morning before Matt had to appear in court, he hitched his horse to the buggy and he and Lillie went to Ardmore. The compromise haunted Lillie because she had to miss worship that morning. She had vowed never to miss unless she was too sick to go or some of the family needed her. Wrestling with her conscience, she asked herself if Matt really needed her on this trip. He was certain he didn't but she thought he did. Handling the actual testimony posed no problem for him but she worried about his spirit. Only week before last he had been in a deep funk. This past week while he traded for the acreage and helped Ben get a loan, he had seemed like himself most of the time. But, at night when they lay side by side, he had kept his own counsel before he went to sleep. The leg jerks began as he drifted off to sleep and disturbed him until he startled awake, turned over and fell asleep more deeply.

Matt kept his attention on the road—clicking to the horse, and adjusting the lines as if driving demanded close watching every minute. Two weeks of dry weather had given the county time to grade the main roads and traffic consisted of one other vehicle in the first five miles. He just doesn't want to talk, she thought. Well, I have problems of my own to work out.

But she was no closer to resolving her conflicts when the road dipped to a shallow creek shortly after the sun reached its zenith. Matt let the horse drink while she opened the basket of food she had prepared for the two or three days they expected to be gone. After he led the animal out of the road, they walked around to loosen their cramped muscles while they ate. She offered Matt an apple.

"We'd better be on our way," he said. "This time of year it'll be nearly dark when we get to Ardmore. I'll walk up the creek and get us some fresh water to drink. We can eat the apples while we travel."

They continued on their silent way until Lillie could stand it no longer. "Matt," she said, "I've been waiting for a chance for us to talk without the children interrupting us or some chore demanding our attention. I haven't told you why I wanted to come with you for this hearing. I know you didn't want me to and I do appreciate your changing your mind."

Matt sat stonefaced staring straight ahead.

Lillie put her hand on his arm. "Matt, look at me!"

The exasperated tone of her voice must have penetrated. He swiveled his whole upper body toward her.

"You've been so torn up over Paul's death that I didn't want to burden you with my feelings but I have prayed for the day when I could confront his murderers face to face. I didn't know how that could happen because I'm scared to death of them. So when I heard that they are actually prisoners and will have to appear in court, I knew it was my chance. But I'm still scared of them and, now that I'm actually on the road, I don't know whether I should have come or not."

She turned to look at him. His face was contorted; he was doing his best to hold back tears. An anguished cry burst from her and she saw him tremble as he transferred the lines to his right hand and drew her close. She buried her face in his shoulder as a great flood of grief overwhelmed her. Matt's body shook with violent sobs. They clung together as they had not done in years until their sudden storm of emotion had subsided.

Lillie sat up straight and smoothed her disheveled hair while Matt fished in a pocket for his handkerchief and wiped his face and blew his nose. Digging around in the food basket, Lillie pulled out a jar of water and they both drank from it.

"My little Lillie," Matt said, "I haven't stood by you through all this grief. I thought only of myself. I'm sorry."

Lillie patted his leg. "No, no, don't blame yourself. I could see that you had more than you could bear. You reminded me of myself when Terence died. I went over the edge then; I couldn't help it. I think the same thing happened to you in all this trouble."

"But I'm a man. I should have been stronger."

"Sometimes, Matt, what happens to us is bigger than we are; man, woman, or child, it doesn't matter. I think this time I withstood trouble better. At least, I didn't have the same breakdown as before."

Matt slapped the horse with the lines but said nothing.

Lillie gathered her courage and said, "Matt, I have a confession to make to you. Ever since Betsy was born, I have felt within myself that I'm not going to have any more of my spells. I didn't tell anyone because at first I waited to be sure. But as I cared for that little doll of a girl, I felt peace abiding in me. I'm ashamed that I have gone for five years without letting you and the family know. I laid around and let Flora do work that I should have been up doing."

At the mention of Flora's name, she felt rather than saw Matt stiffen. She had been looking at her hands in her lap all the time she had been talking. But now she raised her head and turned to him. "Matt, let's get everything between us out in the open on this trip. We haven't been alone together for a few days like this ever in our married life. I want to talk about Buford and Paul, but I want to talk about Flora and Jed, too. Matt, I've loved you since that first day when I saw you and Terence together and I still love you with all my heart. But ever since I had my breakdown, we haven't been close. We skirted issues because we thought we would hurt each other. I'm asking you not to do that any longer and I promise I will be open and truthful with you."

It was a long speech for Lillie and she felt drained. Waiting for Matt to reply, she twisted her handkerchief into a rope, smoothed it out against her lap, and refolded it.

Finally he said, "You know I find it hard to spill my feelings, but I'll try."

They drove on in silence. Shadows lengthened and chill of night seeped into their bones before they saw the lights of Ardmore. Matt turned off Main Street onto Caddo and into the wagon yard. After making arrangements for the horse and buggy, they carried their luggage and the food basket across the street to a hotel.

"Do you have a dining room?" Matt asked when he registered.

"No, but the rooming house on Broadway will still be serving at this hour. You go north to the corner and turn left."

Lillie felt excitement grow as they deposited their things in the room and tidied their appearance. She felt like a young girl again stepping out with her beau. Only this time we won't have a chaperone, she thought. She wanted to take Matt's hand as they walked the short blocks but she knew how embarrassed he would be.

At the boarding house, the owner showed them to a dining room centered with a large table. A turntable in the middle of the table groaned with food. Several men and women at the table stared at them as they entered. One of the women smiled and said, "Here's two empty chairs next to me." Looks like we have our chaperones, Lillie thought.

She had hoped that Matt would be ready to talk when they returned to their room. He had been his old congenial self at the table, talking with the strangers courteously, exchanging names and occupations. But he undressed quickly in the unheated room as she turned the covers down and soon lay snuggled in their warmth.

"Come on to bed," he said.

She blew out the light and, shy as a bride, undressed in the dark. Matt laughed. What a good sound, she thought. It's been too long since I heard it. She crawled into the bed and laid her cold feet on his legs.

He laughed again. "You're cold as a frog. Cuddle against me. I'll warm you up."

When they entered the dining room at the boarding house the next morning, they felt right at home. Only the woman who had offered them a seat the previous night lingered at breakfast.

"Everyone else has already gone to work," she said. "I clerk at Westheimer and Daube, but it's just around the corner and it doesn't take me long to get there. Help yourself; coffee is on the stove. Trudie will come in right away to see how you want your eggs cooked."

After breakfast, they walked the short distance to the Federal Building where the District Court convened. Stump and Abby sat on one of the benches in the hall outside the courtroom. Abby cradled her sleeping baby in her arms.

After greeting them, Matt said, "Lillie, you sit here with the McIntoshes while I go see if I can get permission for you to go into the courtroom when I testify."

Lillie sat sideways on the bench facing Abby. "May I hold him?" she asked. "If he'll let me, I can keep him out here while you testify. Where's Ray?"

Abby handed her the baby. He stirred but quickly settled down. "We left him with Polly, but the baby is still too little to do without me. I don't know how Ray will be without us, but we didn't know what else to do."

Lillie let her body sway in a soothing rhythm. How good it felt to hold a little baby again. She hadn't realized how much she missed it. "He'll be just fine. Flora is keeping Betsy for me. The two children will have a fine time together."

She hadn't noticed Matt's return. When she followed Stump's gaze and turned to look down the hall toward Matt, she thought from his expression that he had overheard her last remark. Oh, dear, she thought, now he knows I went behind his back again.

Matt dropped to the bench on the other side of his former landlord. "They're about ready to get started. This case against them for murder is the first one on the docket. After that they plan to present testimony on the theft case. I hope they are indicted on both counts, but I don't know. We'll just have to wait and see."

Before the hearing started, Mr. Bryce came in and sat beside Matt. The men carried on a quiet conversation and, when Abby seemed disinclined to talk, Lillie became lost in her own thoughts.

So far Matt had not kept his promise to "spill his feelings" as he called it. She had waited for him to broach the subject, but truth to tell, she had seen no good time for a long talk, either. They had both been tired from the jolting buggy trip, and after their sweet coming together again, they had both fallen asleep. Today's hearing had engaged their thoughts and neither of them had been talkative.

The door of the courtroom opened and Territorial Sheriff Pickens and Deputy Timmons came out and spoke to them before they departed down the hall. An official called Mr. Bryce to testify. Abby whispered to Lillie, "I don't know when they'll call me. I'd better feed the baby so he'll be more satisfied while I'm gone." Her unashamed baring of her breast embarrassed Lillie. I wish I had a cloth to cover her with, she thought, as she turned her head.

Mr. Bryce wasn't gone long. They called Matt next. He took her hand and drew it through his bent arm as they walked between the rows of spectators. He found her a seat as far from the defendants as he could. Both of them turned and stared full face at them. After she was seated, she had a view of their profiles. Repulsed but drawn by curiosity, she studied them. The men looked like brothers with their dark unkempt hair, low foreheads, and bulbous noses. One of them appeared to be about the age of her older boys but the other must have been ten years older. Clenched jaws emphasized the deep-set lines in his weather-beaten face.

She had never been in a courtroom before. When she tore her attention away from the defendants, she examined the impressive appointments. The low railing that divided the visitor's area from the court repeated the pattern of walnut paneled walls that reached to high ceilings. All the furniture from the high paneled judge's bench to tables and chairs to the polished hardwood chair she sat in matched the glowing wood of the walls. Impressive as the room itself, the judge in his somber black robes with his solemn expression moved her to awe. Surely the most hardened criminal must quake in his boots when facing such a powerful man in this dramatic setting.

She watched Matt stride forward, raise his right hand and swear. His erect carriage and quick movements belied his years. And when he began to recount the story of finding his son's body, his years in law enforcement provided him with a detached tone although Lillie saw his handlebar moustache shake the slightest bit and knew his lip trembled.

She watched the brothers throughout Matt's testimony. They sat stony-faced and unmoving. She couldn't see for the life of her how her Buford had gotten mixed up with such hard characters. She remembered instances that showed how tenderhearted Buford could be, especially with her and his sisters. Her heart ached for her son and she wondered where he was and if she would ever see him again.

Matt's testimony ended and they left the courtroom. Abby shifted her sleeping baby into Lillie's arms when they called her. He woke almost instantly and sensed that a stranger held him. At first he cried quietly as Lillie tried to soothe him, but soon his bawling became so loud that Lillie was afraid his mother could hear him. She got up and walked down the corridor away from the courtroom bouncing him and crooning. She offered him a sugar tit Abby had given her but he spat it out and yelled louder. When Abby burst out the door of the courtroom, Lillie rushed to her with the baby and thought, I've never been so glad to see anyone in my life.

Notified of a break for lunch, they went back to their room where Lillie prepared a meal from the basket they had brought with them. Matt planned to go back for the afternoon session. After the court announced its decision whether to bind the brothers over for trial, they planned to take up their accusation of theft. The listing of that case included Buford and Matt hoped to see the case split so that Buford could be tried separately if they ever caught him.

Lillie decided to take the opportunity to make the rounds of the dry goods stores. Perhaps her new acquaintance at Westheimer and Daube would direct her to other stores after she shopped there. When she returned to their room eager to show her purchases, she found a dejected Matt lying on the bed. Dropping her packages on a chair, she sat on the side of the bed by him and said, "What happened?"

"On the murder case, they found insufficient evidence and didn't indict them," he said. "I've been afraid all along that would happen. My testimony was mostly hearsay and Abby only heard shots and hoofbeats. She didn't see anything and neither did I. In the other case, they did separate Buford out and kept the Sextons in jail. We might as well get ready and go home early in the morning."

They ate a light supper in their room and went to bed at dark. Lillie had trouble going to sleep and knew that Matt lay awake beside her. It seemed like a good opportunity to have the talk he had promised her but she didn't know how to bring it up and he didn't say anything. She knew better than to try to force him to open up but she found it frustrating.

Eventually they both slept and, when Matt awoke at four o'clock he shook her awake. She dressed and packed while he went across to the wagon yard to get their rig ready. Then they faced a cold north wind on the way to the boarding house for a good hot breakfast where they bid a friendly goodbye to their new acquaintances before heading home.

CHAPTER 27

Matt

The heavy jeans quilt that Lillie had brought along felt good tucked across their laps and wrapped around their legs and feet. He had chuckled as she packed so many clothes for such a short trip but she had reminded him that you never could tell what kind of weather to look for in Oklahoma this time of year. Now he relished the warmth of his old sheepskin lined coat as the north wind whistled around the flaps of the buggy.

"Are you warm enough, Lillie?" he asked.

"Yes, I have this wool shawl pulled tight around my coat. It feels pretty good." She smiled at him, her old happy smile from days gone by.

"Maybe it will warm up when the sun gets a little higher. This black buggy will hold the heat." He filled the time with inconsequential chatter while he got up courage to talk about the four children who had caused them so much grief. He didn't know how to start but he had made her a promise and putting it off wouldn't make it any easier. Lillie seemed to be waiting calmly for him to speak but he knew her too well. She was uneasy inside and anxious to have everything out in the open, as she had said.

Abruptly, he said, "Which one do you want to talk about first?"

She didn't hesitate. "Jed. I want to know all about what happened the day he got married. I have so many questions. Tell me everything."

Where to start? "You know Jed and Ben and I were harvesting corn that day. You and the girls had gone to that quilting bee and Holt was in school. Well, along about dinnertime, Hiram Wade rode up on his horse and reined him right in front of Jed. Then he pulled his shotgun out of the saddle holster and laid it across in front of him. I could see how serious this affair might turn out, so I walked over and invited Wade to state his business."

Matt looked at Lillie and saw tension in every line of her body. I don't know whether she needs to know all the conversation or not, he thought. I'll clean it up for her at the very least.

"Wade didn't waste any words. He said, 'I come after your son here to marry my daughter.' I was afraid to take my eyes from him the mood he was in, so I asked Jed, 'What do you know about this?'

"Jed didn't deny it. In fact, he didn't say a word but guilt was written all over his face. Wade let out an oath. I've heard some as bad in my day but none worse. He told us that no matter what Jed said about it there was going to be a wedding that day.

"I told him Jed was underage so I would have to sign for him if that happened. He was a hard man to deal with but I finally convinced him to meet us in town at the deputy clerk's house. I gave him my word that I would bring Jed and he agreed to go home and get his daughter."

Tears ran down Lillie's cheeks unchecked. In a choked voice, she said, "So he believed you and went home?"

"I told you I gave him my word."

"What did Jed do?"

"He cried and begged me not to make him marry that girl. Lillie, that just tore my heart out. I asked him if there was any possibility the child could be his."

"What did he say?"

"You didn't know it, but I had asked him once before. I knew he had something on his mind and, when I heard about the girl appearing at the dance and them leaving together, I suspicioned this very thing. But he denied it then. So I asked him again and he admitted the possibility."

"Possibility? Is that enough to ruin his life over?"

"That's been eating at me ever since. But I didn't see what else I could do. I had given Wade my word because he might have shot Jed. I just didn't know for sure that he wouldn't. He's high tempered; I could tell. So I told Jed to get dressed for his wedding and I went in and put on my good clothes."

Lillie swiped at her face with a gloved hand. Matt pulled his handkerchief from his pocket and handed it to her. "He left a note for Esther," she said.

"Yes, he asked me to let him at least do that. Lillie, I've never felt so sorry for anyone in my life. He knew we didn't want the girl here, so he packed his clothes and took his gun and his horse." Matt strangled on the last words. Lillie put her arms around him and laid her head on his shoulder. They cried together while the horse plodded on.

Lillie handed his handkerchief back to him. He wiped his eyes and blew his nose. "You know, Lillie, the girl wasn't as bad as I expected. She had on a faded-out dress but it was starched and ironed. She smelled of lye soap from a fresh bath and shampoo. Her hair had a shine to it. I could tell the wedding meant a lot to her and I think she loves Jed. Maybe it will work out. He's not the first man that got a girl in trouble and had to suffer the consequences."

He couldn't tell whether his explanation satisfied Lillie or not. She didn't say anything, but before long she rummaged in the basket and brought out two apples, which she polished on her shawl before handing one to him. Before she could bite into hers, he got out his pocketknife and handed it to her. "You'll have to peel mine," he said. "My teeth won't handle skin anymore."

After she handed it back to him, he savored a bite and said, "These sure are good apples Flora gave us, aren't they?"

She turned and gave him a surprised look. He chuckled. "I notice a few things," he said.

She smiled then. "What else have you noticed?"

"Oh, that everybody in the family sees Flora but me. You see her at church and Ben goes over to the Wilson house pretty often. Makes me wonder if he has his eye on Polly. But I haven't heard her name mentioned around me once. Even little Betsy's careful about that. Am I such an ogre that you are all afraid of me?"

"Well, Matt, you stated your case pretty forcefully. It's just that you are the head of the household and we all want to obey you. Ben goes to see his sister. You know how close they've always been. I think he likes her husband, too. No, it's not Polly he has his eye on."

Who, then? Matt wondered.

But Lillie hadn't finished. "Are you saying you want to make up with her?"

"I've been reconsidering lately. In all this dealing we've had with Stump McIntosh, I've found him to be fair. I always liked Plez and Polly. It's hard to change my ways at my age. I don't know whether I can or not."

"Can do what? Change your ways or make up with your daughter?"

"Change my ways. I'd like to make up with her and Plez if they'll let me."

Lillie hugged him so hard that he almost jerked the horse to a stop.

"One other thing I forgot to tell you," he said. "Yesterday when I went back to the hearing, Stump was there. He told me that they're going to let Plez and Flora live in their house when they go back to Southeast Oklahoma. I told him I'd like to buy that place but just didn't have the money at this time and he said he wouldn't sell it as long as Plez needed it. Then he promised to give me or Ben first chance for it unless Plez wants to buy it sometime in the future."

Lillie's voice had the lilt he liked to hear. "You mean Flora will be just across the woods from us? Why, even Betsy can run over there by herself."

Matt said dryly, "She may feel like it's her second home after staying with Flora while we've been gone."

"You have noticed a lot of things," Lillie said.

Somehow they had returned to the give and take that had always been natural in their relationship. Maybe Lillie was right when she wanted to get things out in the open.

When she started talking, hesitantly and choosing her words carefully, he realized that she actually did want to be above board about many things. "Matt," she said, "I have a confession to make to you. No, it's more than one confession. All these years I haven't been the wife to you that I could have been. At first, I hid behind my grief when Terence died. I don't mean when I had the breakdown. After I came out of it and was at myself most of the time, I let you bear the load of raising the children."

He tried to stop her with a wave of his hand, but she shook her head. "Let me say my piece. It's borne on my conscience far too long. I excused myself by thinking that you would do a better job. I felt like such a failure when I lost him. He'd been my responsibility—mine alone for the first five years of his life—and I couldn't even keep him alive." The depth of her feeling expressed in her broken words twisted his heart and he felt tears dampen his eyes.

She crossed her arms across her chest and grasped her upper arms as if to hold herself together and continued. "So I let you train the children and discipline them while I shirked my duty. I think that was the reason I had spells every once in a while; I felt guilty. And I didn't try to control myself. I could feel the whole family walking on eggs around me—protecting me—and I got to where I liked it."

Matt couldn't believe what he was hearing. He knew she wasn't as bad as she pictured herself but some scenes from the past that confirmed her account flashed before his eyes. There were times when she shut herself in their room and went to bed leaving him to settle an argument between two children or to stop the bleeding and bind up a wound. He had always felt that those things belonged to a mother's tender care. But, fumble-fingered and too sharp-tongued, he had stumbled through. And, over the years, he learned from his mistakes and, if he did say so himself, raised a good brood of children. Except for Buford, who had always been a handful.

Lillie went on in a musing tone of voice. "At first, I felt like such a failure when Terence died that I was afraid of making the same mistakes with my other children. I loved them so much and I could see that you were a good father, but now I see that I didn't treat you right." She began to cry. "Can you ever forgive me?"

Matt placed his hand on top of hers and started to say, 'Yes, of course,' but stopped and thought about it. She deserved more than a pat answer; after all, she had said she wanted to get things out in the open.

He cleared his throat. "Lillie, the first five years of our marriage were the happiest of my life. Combining our two households, building up our herd of cattle, and watching the little ones come along made my life a joy. I'd stop and think, 'What more could a man want?' I had the prettiest, sweetest wife in the county and three little boys."

"Those years seemed perfect to me, too." Lillie squeezed his hand. "But then Terence took sick and died so suddenly and I had that breakdown."

"That was the hardest time. I felt so inadequate; I don't know what I'd have done without your sisters' help. After you got better things smoothed out somewhat. But it's never been the same; we've never been the pair we were before. We had a lot of good times and not too many rough spots until just lately but it could have been better if we'd faced everything together." He cast about in his mind how to make her understand what a burden he had borne in the last several weeks. In a tired voice, he said, "Lillie, I finally felt like I'd had all I could take, especially after I made Jed marry that girl."

Matt listened to the soft clip-clop of the horse's hooves on the dirt road and felt the warmth from the sunshine on the black buggy. They had reached the creek where they had stopped and rested on Sunday. He pulled off the road and jumped out of the buggy. Offering Lillie his hand, he said, "Let's eat a bite and stretch."

She spread a quilt on the sandy creek bank out of the wind while he lifted the basket of food out of the buggy. He unhitched the horse, led him to water, and dipped a bucketful to carry back to go with dinner. Lillie had prepared most of the remaining food and placed it in the center of the quilt. He sat on the quilt across from her and waited for her to hand food to him. But he saw that she had her hands folded in her lap and realized that she expected him to return thanks for the meal.

It had been so long since he had worded a prayer aloud that he searched his mind for the beginning of his standard table prayer. But when the first words formed on his tongue, the balance of the prayer flowed naturally: "We thank thee, Heavenly Father, for the food we are about to receive. Bless it, we pray, to the nourishment of our bodies and us to thy service." He found that he couldn't end the blessing in his usual way; he hadn't finished. Fervently, he added, "And forgive us our sins. In Jesus name, Amen."

When he raised his head and looked at Lillie, he saw tears in her eyes. She got up, almost tripping on her long skirt, and came and knelt beside him. Putting her arms around him, she said, "Forgive me, my dearest."

Crying, he pulled her to him and held her tightly. "There's much to forgive on both sides, my little Lillie. If I ever had anything against you, I forgive it and ask you to do the same for me. Let's wipe the slate clean and go from here facing our life together as a unit. Agreed?"

"Oh, yes, yes," she said.

He looked at her joyous face and kissed it. "Now, if we're going to get home by dark, we'd better eat and get on the road."

In 1906 Matt Conover moved his family of ten from Texas to Indian Territory to keep his son Buford out of jail. A year later Ben returns from Texas to help his family through the winter before he departs for Texas to live. That night he meets Esther McMasters and falls in love at first sight before he discovers she is his brother Jed's sweetheart. But Jed has other problems that impact both Ben and Esther.

Buford hasn't quit his criminal ways and, before the night is over, one brother lies dead from ambush and the family is thrown into such turmoil that Matt is afraid it will send his frail wife, Lillie, back into deep depression. As each adult in the family copes with grief differently, Matt says, "This move up here was probably the worst decision I ever made in my life."

Family Saga
Oklahoma
Pioneer
True to Life

A realistic representation of frontier life and death, murder and punishment as it affects an Oklahoma pioneer family.

Voncille Shipley was raised in Healdton, a town near the area depicted in her first novel, *This Raw, Red Land*. Today she lives in South Central Oklahoma not many miles from that location. She and her husband, John, have an acreage on which they raise pecans and hay.

0-595-27136-7

Printed in the United States
17455LVS00003B/286-294